Each second that ticked by without finding his son was another second closer to losing him forever.

However, at Darcy's look of disappointment, he said, "But I think there's enough food to scrounge up something decent, at least for tonight. Do you cook?"

"Not really," she admitted. "My mom always did the cooking. Her love language was food. When I was sick, she'd make fresh chicken noodle. To even suggest something from a can was an insult. She would've made my school lunches for me until I graduated if I hadn't put my foot down."

Rafe heard a hint of sadness in the deprecating laugh, but he didn't press even though he was curious. It was best to keep the lines drawn to avoid emotional entanglements. To know too much was an invitation to want more.

Like tangled sheets and rumpled clothing.

* * *

Dear Reader,

I've always wanted to participate in a continuity project, so when I was asked to be one of the six authors for the "Perfect" romantic-suspense project, I was nearly giddy with excitement. What a joyful experience, collaborating with such talented authors. I learned a lot about myself as a writer, and about working as a team on what is usually a solitary endeavor.

If you're following the series (you don't want to miss any of these amazing connected stories!) you're in for a thrilling adventure. This book, the third in the series, follows Dr. Rafe Black straight into the heart of a twisted cult as he searches undercover for his missing son. He's playing a dangerous game, pretending to be a Devotee, but he isn't alone. Darcy Craven is searching for answers and she won't let anything stop her—not even when her life is threatened.

I love characters who are driven by an internal force and push forward in spite of the obstacles in their way. It was a treat to delve into the scary world of a cult master. I hope you enjoy my vision of Perfect, Wyoming, and all the players in this most dangerous and thrilling game!

Hearing from readers is a special joy. Please feel free to drop me a line via email through my website at www.kimberlyvanmeter.com or through snail mail at Kimberly Van Meter, P.O. Box 2210, Oakdale, CA 95361.

Kimberly

Watch out for these other books in the riveting new Perfect, Wyoming miniseries:

Special Agent's Perfect Cover by Marie Ferrarella—*January 2012*

Rancher's Perfect Baby Rescue by Linda Conrad—*February 2012*

Lawman's Perfect Surrender by Jennifer Morey—*April 2012*

The Perfect Outsider by Loreth Anne White—*May 2012*

Mercenary's Perfect Mission by Carla Cassidy—*June 2012*

KIMBERLY VAN METER

A Daughter's Perfect Secret

ROMANTIC *SUSPENSE*

Special thanks and acknowledgment to Kimberly Van Meter for her contribution to the Perfect, Wyoming miniseries.

Recycling programs
for this product may
not exist in your area.

ISBN-13: 978-0-373-27766-7

A DAUGHTER'S PERFECT SECRET

www.Harlequin.com

Printed in U.S.A.

Books by Kimberly Van Meter

Harlequin Romantic Suspense

‡*Sworn to Protect* #1666
‡*Cold Case Reunion* #1669
A Daughter's Perfect Secret #1696

Silhouette Romantic Suspense

To Catch a Killer #1622
Guarding the Socialite #1638

Superromance

The Truth About Family #1391
*Father Material #1433
**Return to Emmett's Mill* #1469
A Kiss to Remember #1485
**An Imperfect Match* #1513
**Kids on the Doorstep* #1577
**A Man Worth Loving* #1600
**Trusting the Bodyguard* #1627
***The Past Between Us* #1694
***A Chance in the Night* #1700
***Secrets in a Small Town* #1706

‡Native Country
*Home in Emmett's Mill
**Mama Jo's Boys

Other titles by this author available in ebook format.

KIMBERLY VAN METER

wrote her first book at sixteen and finally achieved publication in December 2006. She writes for Harlequin Superromance and Harlequin Romantic Suspense. She and her husband of seventeen years have three children, three cats and always a houseful of friends, family and fun.

As always, to my friends and family. They keep me grounded and present when I have a tendency to drift. I love you all!

Chapter 1

Three months ago...

Rafe Black couldn't still his fingers. A pile of tiny bits of shredded paper from his straw wrapper betrayed his nerves as he checked his watch one last time.

Abby was officially one hour late.

"Another tea?" The waitress, young, fresh-faced and clearly trying to earn a good tip, smiled in earnest until she saw the mess on his table. "You got something on your mind?" she asked, gesturing to the paper pile.

He didn't want to be rude, but his thoughts were narrowed to a point and there wasn't much room for chitchat. "No more tea," he said, sending the hint he wasn't up for sharing but then added to soften the brush-off, "Thank you, though."

The waitress nodded and scooped up his pile with a small smile. "Just holler if you do."

He rubbed his forehead, massaging the tension pulling on his brows and bunching the muscles in his neck. Where was Abby? They'd agreed to meet here, at this grubby diner about forty miles outside of Cold Plains, Wyoming, following a hurried and frantic phone call from Abby after she'd dropped a bomb on him.

If Abby were to be believed, she'd given birth to his son only months earlier, and now they were both in danger.

Had she been lying? His gut told him no. He'd heard the fear in her voice. Felt the terror even from across the telephone line. Which was why, when she'd sent him a photograph of the boy—a damn spitting image of him with his dark hair and eyes and Abby's cupid-bow mouth—and begged him to wire $10,000 to a Western Union in Laramie, he hadn't hesitated. He simply went to his savings account, made the withdrawal and then persuaded Abby to meet him here—today.

The money had been picked up, but Abby was conspicuously absent. He'd be a liar if he didn't admit to some misgivings. Had she taken the money and split? Maybe.

The fact of the matter was, and this was a bit of an embarrassment, he didn't know Abby well. Only well enough to father a child after a torrid one-night stand that'd been completely out of character for him.

Damn. He pulled the photograph from his wallet and stared at the child's image. Had he been played? A cynic would say, wholeheartedly, yes. But he recognized his own features on that child's face, and he couldn't walk away. Even if Abby hadn't called, terrified and sobbing, he wouldn't have been able to walk away. That went against everything he believed in, stood for. And so, here he sat, like a chump, waiting for a woman who had plainly stood him up.

He flagged the waitress, tossing a ten-dollar bill on the table. Her eyes lit up at the generous tip, but then she bit her lip as if pinged by conscience. "That's too much of a tip for just an ice tea," she admitted.

He pushed the bill toward her but handed her a business card, too. "I need a favor," he said, hating that he had no idea what had happened to Abby and his son.

She pocketed the ten and accepted the card, her expression wary. "Sure. What can I do for you?" She glanced at the card, reading, "Rafe Black, M.D. A doctor, huh?"

"Yes," he answered with a brief smile. "I was waiting for a friend. Her name is Abby Michaels and she has a three-month-old baby boy. If she happens to show up, please give her my card. It's very important that I talk to her. Can you do that for me?"

She nodded. "Sure. Is she okay?"

"I hope so," he said. God, he hoped so. He rose. "Thank you. I appreciate your help."

"No problem," she said. "I hope your friend is okay."

He answered with a smile as tight as the grip on his heart and walked out of the diner, but in his gut, he knew something was terribly wrong.

It wasn't long before he discovered he'd been right.

Abby Michaels was dead. Rafe pushed his fingers through his hair, that damnable tremble returning to his hands, betraying everything he was doing to remain calm and in control. He should've stayed, should've reported her missing. Maybe they might've found her before… He suppressed a racking shudder and tried to focus on the here and now, but it wasn't as if he had any experience with this sort of thing and there was so much at stake. He straightened and leaned forward, dread and anxiety twisting his gut in knots.

"And how did you find out about the victim's death?" the stone-faced detective Victor Reynolds asked, looking up from his paperwork, staring a hole into Rafe.

"I caught something on the news about five murdered women, and Abby was one of them. I was shocked," he said, but shock was too mild of a word for what he was feeling. More like reeling from a nightmare that he couldn't escape. After the news report, it'd taken him a full minute to fully comprehend the enormity of the situation. Abby was dead; what about his son? "I knew she was in some kind of trouble but I had no idea it was this bad. Listen, there's something else, she had a child. Was she alone when she was found? The news report didn't say."

"No." Reynolds's gaze narrowed sharply. "What child?"

"She called me earlier in the week, saying she'd had my child, a son she named Devin," he admitted, the grit in his eye burning from the lack of sleep. He'd driven straight through from Colorado Springs to this little hole-in-the-wall place outside of Laramie, where Abby's body had been found earlier that day. He'd shortened the nearly four-hour drive into three; it was a damn miracle he'd arrived alive. "She told me to meet her at this little diner, some greasy-spoon place about forty miles south from here," he said. "But she never showed. I should've known something went wrong."

"How well did you know the victim?"

"Not well," he said, embarrassed by his admission. He wasn't the kind to sleep around, but he'd met Abby while away at a medical conference in the hotel bar. One thing had led to another and before he'd known it, they'd stumbled to his room for drunken sex. Not his finest hour, for sure, and one he hadn't planned to ever repeat. "We had a one-night stand a little over a year ago. I hadn't seen or heard from her since, until she called saying she was in some kind of danger and needed money."

"And you sent it to her?"

He nodded. "Ten thousand."

At that, Detective Reynolds paused, speculation in his flat, squinty eyes. "Ten large, eh? That's a lot of money to send to a virtual stranger."

"She wasn't out to scam me. I heard the fear in her voice. She was terrified."

"Some women are good actresses," Reynolds said with a subtle shrug. "You believed it was your kid before a paternity test?"

"Yes," he said, growing angry at the detective's implication that Abby had duped him for some reason. This was starting to feel like less of a good idea as he sat across the table from the detective. "Let's get to the point. There's a woman dead, and her child is missing. Are you going to put out an Amber Alert or am I going to have to go up the ladder for some results?"

"Cool your jets, hotshot," Reynolds said, his tone hard. "Of course we'll issue an Amber Alert but let me tell you what I'm seeing.... Motive."

"Motive?" Rafe stared, unable to fathom what the hell the detective was getting at. "What kind of motive?"

Reynolds leaned back in his chair, his gaze never leaving Rafe, watching his every move as if Rafe was some kind of deranged killer who might jump for his throat at any minute. "Maybe you're pissed that she duped you for a kid that wasn't yours? Ten large is a lot of money. But then, I hear doctors make good money. Better than cops, that's for sure."

Rafe ignored that. "He's my son. I don't need a paternity test to confirm what I see with my eyes—that he looks just like me. And what kind of killer drives four hours to the police station to help identify the body and then leaves a DNA sample?" he asked in disgust. "You need to look into the last place Abby was before she was killed. The news report said the one thing the murdered women had in common was this place called Cold Plains."

Reynolds grunted. "Nice place. Ever been there?"

"No." He bit back his irritation at the man. "Does the name Samuel Grayson mean anything to you?"

"Should it?"

"I don't know," Rafe said, frustration getting the best of him. "But Abby...she was running from this Cold Plains.... I did some looking around, and I guess this Samuel guy runs the town. Maybe you ought to ask around, do some actual investigative work," he muttered under his breath.

"I don't tell you how to be a doctor—how about you zip your lip when it comes to police work?" Reynolds growled, bristling at the insult. But he relented, as if realizing Rafe's suggestion had merit, and said, "I know a guy in Cold Plains, Bo Fargo. He'll know if there's something hinky going down in his town. I'll make some inquiries," he said then slid a card across the table. "We'll be in touch. If a child turns up and he matches your DNA profile, we'll call. In the meantime, don't do anything rash like leave the country."

It was everything Rafe could do to keep a civil tongue. He'd get no satisfaction from the local law enforcement; that much was abundantly clear. They were too busy eyeing him for the crime rather than chasing down any real leads. Abby had been shot, execution style, in the back of the head, and then her body had been dumped in a wooded area. If a hunter hadn't come across her body, likely the wildlife would've taken care of any evidence left behind. If he wanted answers, he'd have to find them himself.

He was going to Cold Plains.

Ah hell, a voice in his head said, worrying about the everyday details of his life—his practice and his patients, mostly—but all he had to do was pull that picture and stare into those baby eyes and know none of that mattered until that boy was safe. Tears stung his eyes and he blinked them away, focusing to a narrow point out of necessity. If he allowed himself to slip into the fear that ate away at his control, he'd lose whatever edge he might have that could help him find his son.

Who are you kidding? You're not a cop, man, the voice intruded again. *Leave it to the professionals.*

Professionals like Detective Reynolds with his cold eyes and ignorant small-town disposition? Not a chance. He was a smart man, capable of figuring a few things out on his own. He wished he'd known more about Abby. Why hadn't he tried to find her after that night? They'd had good chemistry. Her soft laugh had been like a warm caress. Or maybe he'd just been really drunk. No, that couldn't have been it entirely. Abby had had something special. The only reason he hadn't pursued her after that night was because of his single-minded career focus. Well, that, and the discomfort of having to tell people that they'd met in a bar and hooked up after tequila shots. He scrubbed his face, pushing away the sting of guilt. Now wasn't the time for that—he'd have plenty of time to twist with remorse after his son was found. *If* he was found. No, don't think like that. He would find him. That was a promise.

Until then, he had to be ruthless with himself.

And everyone he came into contact with. All that mattered was his son.

Chapter 2

Present day...

Darcy Craven's stare drifted over the familiar items of her childhood, standing in her mother's—scratch that, as of two days ago, *adoptive* mother's—living room, and she wondered how such a big secret had been kept from her.

She was not the biological daughter of Louise Craven but rather the daughter of a woman Darcy had never known existed until today. If she weren't cracking in two from grief over Louise's death, she would've thought she was numb inside. But no, there was a pulsing raw wound inside that gushed each time her heart beat. She'd been lied to, but worse was that her mother had been forced to give her up because she'd been in danger.

She couldn't muster an ounce of anger against Louise, but she wished she had more answers than what she'd been left with.

"I never wanted you to find out, but you need to know," Louise had rasped from her bed, the cancer eating her from the inside out, stealing her breath along with her strength.

"Shhh," Darcy had urged, distressed over how Louise was exerting herself when the doctor had plainly told her to rest. "Whatever it is, it's fine," she said, trying to soothe her. She checked the morphine drip. Louise was dying; there was no coming back from that ledge now that the cancer had metastasized from her pancreas. All they could do was offer her comfort, which was why she was home instead of the hospital, and Darcy wanted to make sure that her mother died in peace. "You need to rest."

"Darcy, honey, I'm dying. We both know that," Louise said, her shoulders shuddering on a cough. "But before I go I have to tell you something that I've been carrying around since the day you came into my life."

At that Darcy stilled, a knot settling in her stomach even as she tried to logically explain away the feeling. The doctors had warned her that the high-octane narcotics could cause erratic behavior. "What are you talking about?" she asked. "In the overall scheme of things, I'm sure it's not as big as you think it is."

"Darcy, *listen,* damn it."

Her mother never cursed. "What's wrong?" Darcy asked, settling to meet her mother's stare.

A single tear oozed out from the corner of Louise's eye, and she appeared to sag into the mattress a little farther, but she rallied with a brief show of strength as she clasped Darcy's hand. "There's a picture in my jewelry box," she started, and Darcy shook her head.

"Mom, I've been in your jewelry box a thousand times. There's no picture," she said.

"There's a false bottom. Open it and bring it to me."

Darcy gaped. A false bottom? That unsettled feeling returned with a vengeance. Her mother was not the sort to hide things in secret. She'd been a PTA mom, for crying out loud. She'd baked cupcakes and cookies for bake sales and had volunteered on the safety patrol. She wasn't the kind of woman who harbored secrets. Yet, here she was, knocking on the bottom drawer to find, yes indeed, it had a false bottom. She gave a gentle tug and the top popped up, revealing a single photograph, aged and yellowed, of a beautiful woman. She flipped it over, but there was nothing written on the back. She returned to her mother. "Is this it?" she asked quizzically, handing the photo to Louise.

Her mother took the photo and stared, her eyes filling. She passed a shaky hand over the image of the smiling young woman, and she closed her eyes, as if seeing the photo brought back painful memories.

"Who is she?" Darcy asked. What was going on? Wasn't there enough tragedy in the Craven household without the added burden of some secret that she was fairly certain she didn't want to know? She maintained a façade of calm, but inside she felt nauseous.

"Your biological mother," Louise answered, that single admission kicking the bottom out from Darcy's world as if the only mother she'd ever known dying from cancer wasn't a big enough blow. "I'm sorry...you were never supposed to find out this way but there's power in knowledge, and my darling sweet girl, you're going to need all the power you can muster to stand up to that man."

"What man?" Darcy asked hollowly, her bewilderment giving way to shock. "What are you talking about? You're my mother. I don't even look like her. This is crazy talk—"

"There isn't a lot of time," Louise cut in, yet was stopped short as a racking cough stole the air from her lungs. Darcy helped her drink some water, but it was several moments before Louise could speak again. Darcy's thoughts were spun out on a surreal setting. Surely this was happening to someone else, not her.

"Darcy, your mother was a good friend of mine even though I was a bit older than she was. Her name was Catherine. She got pregnant at seventeen and entrusted you with me when she had to run. At first I thought she would return, but as the years went on, I realized she wasn't coming back. I raised you as my own, and I couldn't love you more than if I gave birth to you myself." Louise's weak grip on Darcy's hand tightened and Darcy knew her mother wouldn't lie. Still, it was a lot to take in and, frankly, Darcy was not above wanting to shut it all out and forget she'd ever heard it. "There's more," Louise said, the urgency returning to her voice. "Your mother was involved with a very dangerous man. And he's only gotten more influential as time has passed. You might've heard of him. His name is Samuel Grayson."

Darcy startled, the name jumping out at her from a recent news story on rising cult leaders. "That's the man who's running that town outside Laramie? The one who claims he's found the secret to running a perfect society? He's a nut," she said, horrified.

Louise agreed with a weak nod. "The very same. He's got a whole town of followers now, and there's no stopping him when he's got something in his sights. And I'm afraid for you."

"Why? Does he even know about me?"

"I don't know," Louise admitted, a shudder wheezing from her frail chest. "But I couldn't let you face the future without knowing. There's a possibility…that he may have done something to Catherine."

"How do you know?"

"I haven't heard from her in a long time, years, actually."

Darcy swallowed. "You…had contact with her?"

"Not truly, honey. A postcard here and there. Just something to let me know she was all right. I never had an address or a phone number. She was scared that if she was too close to you, he'd find you. She loved you so much, she wanted to make sure you were always safe. But the last postcard came years ago. I'm afraid something happened to her, and the only person who would've had reason to hurt her was Samuel Grayson. You have to promise me you'll stay away from that man. He's evil."

Darcy nodded. At that moment she'd have agreed to anything to ease the torment in her mother's eyes. That was two days ago. And her mother was gone. She was alone.

Something toxic burned in Darcy's chest—a combustible mixture that was equal parts rage and grief with a healthy dose of insatiable need to know the truth about her mother—and she knew she'd lied to Louise.

She had to know where her mother was, had to know if she was safe and she had to know what part Samuel Grayson played in this whole twisted drama that had somehow attached itself to her formerly happy life.

Darcy wanted answers—and nothing was going to stop her.

She shifted in her coach-class airplane seat, wishing she'd had the extra money to spring for at least the business class to accommodate her long legs, but pushed her discomfort aside to take in every detail of her birth mother, Catherine. Even though the picture was more than twenty-two years old, Darcy could tell her mother had been beautiful. If only she'd inherited her fine bone structure, she lamented privately. The only physical attribute she seemed to have been gifted with of her mother's was her blue eyes. She lightly traced a finger down the curve of her mother's cheek, wondering what she'd been thinking when the picture was taken. How had Catherine gotten mixed up with someone like Samuel Grayson? Darcy had unearthed a few news articles on the man. On the surface, he seemed legit, but the cultlike following creeped her out. According to the news clippings, Cold Plains was his utopia. Except everyone knew a utopia was an illusion, so how did Samuel keep everyone happy and playing along? It smacked of an M. Night Shyamalan movie. Where was the freaky twist?

Darcy closed her eyes and tried not to let the grief that hovered on the edges of her sanity creep in. She couldn't lose focus. Any semblance of a normal life had shattered when Louise had dropped her bombshell. And, if the truth were known, chasing after answers kept her from acknowledging her bone-deep grief over Louise's death. It was too soon, too quick. They'd had no time to prepare. The cancer had moved in quickly, without mercy. Before they'd known it, Louise had been given a death sentence. In spite of her closed eyes, a trail of moisture leaked from them, and she wiped it away on her sleeve.

"Are you okay, honey?" the woman next to her asked, a kind expression on her middle-aged face. "I have some tissues if you need some."

Darcy smiled at the kindness. "Thank you. I'm all right. I'm just tired. Stuff's getting to me, I guess."

"Might help if you talk about it. I'm a good listener."

Darcy withheld a sigh. It was a nice offer, but it wasn't as if she could actually share what was going on in her life. She smiled briefly to let the woman know the offer was appreciated but gave a little shake of her head, murmuring her decline.

The woman nodded and let her be. Darcy was thankful for the window seat. At least she could watch the states go by in shades of green, gold and blue as she flew from her cozy world, where everything had once made sense, to her new existence, where danger lurked side by side by the secrets she felt compelled to uncover.

Likely, it was stupid—reckless even—and the very thing Louise had cautioned her against.

But she couldn't stop herself. Maybe there was a slim chance that Catherine was still alive and Darcy could help her.

Then again, maybe Catherine was dead, and Darcy was heading straight into the arms of the man who'd snuffed out her life.

It was a cruel coin flip of possibility.

But she wasn't turning back. Hell no, she wasn't turning back.

Chapter 3

Rafe's smile faded as soon as his last patient walked out the door and climbed into his car, his attention riveted to the man waiting patiently, a seemingly placid expression on his otherwise rugged face.

Rafe locked the door and flipped the sign that said his little practice was closed for the evening, and any emergencies should be directed to the urgent-care clinic. "Any news?" he asked, but by the grim tensing of the man's mouth, Rafe had his answer. "He's here. I know it. That sonofabitch has my son somewhere in this little creepshow of a town, and it's killing me that I've been unable to find out where."

"Keep your voice down," Hawk Bledsoe, an FBI agent who'd grown up in Cold Plains before it became the stomping ground of Samuel Grayson, the man Rafe was sure had Devin hidden somewhere, warned. "You know it's not safe to go running your mouth without consequence. I came to tell you there's someone new in town, and I think as soon as Grayson takes a look at her, he's going to be on her like stink on crap to recruit her as one of his *breeders*."

Rafe grimaced at the crude term that had sprung up at the realization that Grayson fancied himself a matchmaker of sorts and always sought out the best-looking candidates to match up in the hopes that their progeny was equally perfect aesthetically.

"Not my problem," Rafe said, hating himself for being such a cold bastard, but if he worried about every single person who stumbled into Grayson's clutches, he'd go insane. He was here for one reason: to find Devin and then get the hell out.

But in the meantime, he had to play the game. He'd shown up in Cold Plains three months ago, pretending to want to relocate to the picturesque town, even going so far as to appear interested in the ridiculous garbage Grayson preached every day in his seminars—all in the name of finding his son.

It hadn't been as easy as he'd thought when he first started. He figured someone was bound to talk eventually, but Grayson ruled with an iron fist and fear rode shotgun with these people. So far, he'd gotten nowhere. When he discovered that Bledsoe was an undercover FBI agent, he'd been relieved to find someone who wasn't drinking the crazy juice, but thus far, even Bledsoe had come up empty.

"She's young and she needs a job," Bledsoe continued as if Rafe hadn't spoken. "Don't you need a receptionist to handle your phones?"

"I hadn't planned on staying this long," Rafe grumbled, not exactly answering but not denying it, either. True, he was running himself a bit ragged trying to keep his office as self-sufficient as possible, not because he was a control freak, but rather, he needed to be able to trust the people he worked with, and frankly, trust was in short supply in this town.

"How do we even know she's not a Devotee?" Rafe asked, referencing the people who followed Samuel Grayson, marching along like good soldiers in Grayson's utopian army.

"We don't. But this could be a good way to gain some additional insight if she is. If she's not, think of it as good karma points."

Rafe looked away, caught between his urge to protect an innocent person and keep a healthy distance away from anything that might distract him from finding Devin. "How do you know she needs a job?"

"She arrived yesterday. She's staying at the hotel and I heard through the grapevine that she's asking around to see if anyone's hiring. I'll make it known to her that you're looking for a receptionist. Do me a favor and hire her. Do yourself a favor and hire her. You're looking a little frayed around the edges, and you need to stay sharp in this shark tank or you'll get eaten."

Rafe nodded wearily and rubbed at his eyes. "Right. So, still nothing out there about Devin?"

"Not a word. But someone knows something. They're just scared to talk. We'll find him," Bledsoe assured him, and Rafe tried to take comfort in the fact that he wasn't searching alone, but he was no closer to the truth than he was when he'd stepped foot in this town.

Sure, on the surface, Cold Plains looked like a dream come true, the perfect place to settle down and raise kids, but if you scratched the surface of that perfect veneer, a whole lot of *what-the?-Oh-my-God* appeared like dirty bubbles in a stagnant pond.

"Maybe we ought to call in reinforcements, you know? Tell the feds what you know so far… Maybe it's enough for an indictment."

Bledsoe shook his head, the motion definitive. "No. We've got smoke and mirrors when it comes to Grayson. He's popped out of worse, smelling like a rose. He lets others take the fall and then walks away. If we go off half-cocked out of fear and desperation, it'll end badly for everyone. And trust me, the man is not only slippery but dangerous. It wouldn't surprise me if he were to pull the plug on everyone, going down in grand, Waco, Texas, style. We don't want to add to the body count. Stay the course. We'll get him. But in the meantime, just chill and keep doing what you're doing. Grayson likes you. He thinks you're getting ready to pledge. That's good. His guard will be down. Eventually something will slip. That's when we'll find what we're looking for—evidence to take him down—and your son."

Rafe swallowed his emotions. His son. Was he even still alive? Every child he saw on the street that was the same age as his son at this point made him do a double take and wonder. He didn't put it past Grayson to have a child killed—the man had no soul—but Grayson did everything for a purpose. So if Devin was still alive, it was for a reason. And it might be desperate, wishful thinking, but he knew in his heart that Devin was alive somewhere—or maybe it was just that he had to believe that or go crazy.

Darcy had never seen a cleaner street. Usually even the nicest cities and towns had little bits of trash that the street sweeper missed, but not Cold Plains. The dark asphalt looked fresh, newly poured, and the crosswalk paint fairly gleamed. It was as if trash wasn't allowed and anyone who had the audacity to carelessly litter was vigorously dealt with. Darcy shuddered at what her imagination conjured. She'd done a fair amount of homework on Samuel Grayson and Cold Plains before she'd purchased her plane ticket, but there hadn't been a whole lot out there. A Google search had pulled up some historic photos of the town when it was merely a spot in the road, a trading outpost really, and she'd managed to find a few street views from the Google maps, but the town had maintained a rural atmosphere. Certainly charming to the eye at first glance, she thought wistfully. Too bad there was something rotten in Denmark. She adjusted her purse, where her mother's picture lay tucked in her wallet, and set out to wander around, looking every bit the happy-go-lucky tourist.

Somewhere, a deep resonant bonging startled her, and she realized the noise was coming from an impressive three-story building of marble and glass, directly ahead on the main street. A man must've noticed her shock and confusion, because he tapped her on the shoulder with a warm smile. "New to Cold Plains?" the man asked.

"Oh, uh, yes, actually. What's going on?" She motioned to the people starting to file toward the building.

A smile wreathed the man's face. "It's time for the noon session. You're in for a real treat. Do you believe in fate?"

No. Not really. "A little, I think," she lied, curious to see where this fruitloop was headed. "Why?"

"Because fate brought you to Cold Plains. And now you'll find out why. Come." He held his hand out to her, and she wondered if this was how the victims of Jim Jones fell under his charm. All it took was one step.... Well, she was here for answers. She pasted a bright smile on her lips and accepted his hand. He grinned. "You won't regret it. Samuel's sessions are almost magical. So inspiring."

Samuel Grayson... A dangerous chill touched her skin. Time to meet Daddy.

Darcy entered the community center and allowed her awe to show. "Wow, this is some fancy place for such a small town," she said, taking in the huge fresh spray of flowers gracing the entry and the sweet fragrance they gave off. "Who pays for all this?" she wondered out loud.

"Needs are met as they are needed," the man said by way of answer, which to Darcy's mind wasn't much of an answer at all. Maybe the man was a politician. He directed her to an empty seat. "Enjoy and be transformed."

And then he melted into the crowd, which was okay by Darcy, because truthfully, the guy was creeping her out more than a little. Maybe it was because she wasn't accustomed to such overt polite behavior from total strangers, or maybe she was just more of a city girl than a country girl and didn't know how to react when someone wasn't flipping her off or stealing her cab. Either way, she was happy to sit and simply observe unnoticed for the time being.

She scanned the crowd and immediately noted a striking commonality: it was the congregation of beautiful people.

Not a single unattractive person milled about. So much for diversity, she thought uneasily. It was probably an odd coincidence. How could a whole town be comprised of models?

She shifted in her seat and a man caught her eye. Of course, like everyone else in the building, he was attractive, but there was something else about him that drew her. Tall, with a lean but solid frame that filled his shirt nicely and narrowed to tight hips, he stood in the back, observing with an eye as keen as her own. An odd flutter tickled her stomach, and she quickly turned away for fear of being caught staring. Everyone in this place was cuckoo, she reminded herself. Even if they were hotter than hell.

A hush fell upon the crowd, and Darcy saw that a man had taken the stage. The man, mesmerizing with his midnight hair, which gleamed in the fluorescent light, flashed incredibly white teeth in a broad, magnanimous grin that immediately caused her to suck in a painfully tight breath. She was looking at her father. No matter that she'd come to find answers and she'd followed the trail to Cold Plains, a part of her had hoped that Louise had been wrong. That her adoptive mother's bedside confession had simply been the unfortunate ramblings of a woman doped up on intense dosages of morphine and not that of a woman harboring a deadly secret. But there was no denying that the enigmatic man captivating the assembled crowd had contributed to her DNA. How did she know for sure? It wasn't some New Agey feeling—no, it was much simpler than that.

She was his spitting image.

Suddenly, everything began to swim, and for the first time in her life, Darcy slid right out of her chair and onto the floor.

She'd fainted.

Chapter 4

Darcy slowly opened her eyes and focused on the blurry face full of concern and struggled to sit up.

"Hold on, you've fainted," a voice, low and soft but distinctly masculine, said. The man smelled of cinnamon, and gave a gentle push on her shoulder to remain lying down. "Are you dizzy? Does your head hurt?"

She covered her eyes with her hand and bit her lip, more mortified than anything else. So much for blending in, stealthlike. Seemed her ninja skills weren't up to par. Not that she'd ever had any.

"Miss?" the voice prompted, causing her to shake her head.

"I'm fine. Just embarrassed." Against the man's direction, she rolled to her side and sat up, realizing she was no longer in the community center. Gone were the marble-accented furniture and glossy floors, replaced with country kitsch and quaint down-home charm. "Um. Where am I?"

She blinked away the fuzziness in her vision and choked back a gasp when she realized the man she'd seen earlier at the community center, the one whom she'd been compelled to stare at, was now staring at her with an air of concern and curiosity. "And…who are you?"

When he smiled, the corners of his mouth lifted but his eyes remained deadly serious, and Darcy found the contradiction unsettling, just like everything else in this place. Except, in spite of that, she couldn't deny there was something about him that made her mouth dry and her thoughts wander.

"My name is Dr. Rafe Black. You passed out at the community center, and you were brought here. It's closer than the urgent-care clinic," he explained, then returned to his diagnostic mode by removing a penlight and shining it in her eyes. She batted it away on instinct. She'd only just recovered her sight, and now she had dots dancing before her eyes. He frowned. "I had to check for a concussion," he said, pocketing the penlight. "And what is your name?"

"Darcy Craven. Nice to meet you. And I slid from my chair, not the roof," she grumbled, highly embarrassed by the whole incident. "Really, I'm fine. Please don't make a fuss. I was very accident-prone as a child, so this is nothing," she said, trying to lighten things up. She didn't like the way her stomach was still doing tiny flutters at being so close to the handsome doctor. There was far more at stake than finding a hot guy to date. Before Louise had gotten sick, Darcy had been a different kind of girl—out for the good time and the fun—but then everything had changed when Louise had needed her. Responsibility had been an uncomfortable fit at first, but she'd quickly adapted when she realized she was all Louise had in the world and vice versa. It'd made her grow up fast. She supposed a part of that irresponsible girl still lived and breathed, because otherwise, how else would she have had the wherewithal to embark on this dangerous quest? Be that as it may, it didn't mean she had to follow every impulse, and that included allowing herself to be attracted to the handsome stranger, who, by the way, was still scrutinizing her every move with that serious stare.

"I'm fine. I promise," she assured him, jumping down from the exam table and edging away. "So, I have insurance.... Do you need me to fill out some forms or something for you to bill for your time?"

He waved away her offer, his brows still knitted together. "No charge. But I still think you ought to take it easy. People don't just faint for no reason, and it's the reason I'm worried about. You could have something serious happening neurologically. Would you object to having some tests run?"

Tests? That smacked of a bad idea. What if this was some ploy to get her DNA for some weird reason? She recognized the paranoia in her thought process, but she supposed that was unavoidable given the circumstances. "No thanks. Not big on tests. Ignorance is bliss sometimes," she said. "So you're the doctor here...the only doctor in the whole town?" she asked, switching subjects.

"No, I'm not the only one. There are a few at the urgent-care facility. However, I am the only one with a private practice on the main street. And how did you find yourself in Cold Plains?" he asked, moving away to fold his arms across his chest, the frowning easing into an expression of congenial friendliness. "Family from here?"

She startled but hid it well. It was a fair question, no need to read anything into it. "Nope, no family here. Just sounded like a great place. It's been getting a fair amount of press lately with all its, uh, attributes of clean living."

"Ah, yes, Cold Plains is a living example of how people can live in harmony," Rafe said, smiling. "There's been a few reporters who've picked up on Cold Plains's charms. I think a few even relocated here after their stories ran. It's a special place."

"Yeah, I'm getting that," she said, nodding. Was he a Grayson follower, too? She wasn't sure. She had to assume he was or why else would he be here? Darcy forced a bright smile. "So, actually, you might be able to help me."

"Oh? How's that?"

"Know of anyone who's hiring? I need a job."

For a split second, she could've sworn a flash of recognition had passed over his expression, but it was gone in a heartbeat, causing her to wonder if she'd seen anything at all.

"What fortuitous timing," he said. "I happen to be looking for a receptionist. How good are you at answering phones and taking appointments?" he asked.

Was he serious? She stared. When he didn't confess he was kidding, she caught her bottom lip and worried it as she considered his offer. A receptionist? For the hot—possibly cuckoo—doctor? On one hand, being the front desk person to the local doctor could put her in contact with a lot of people; on the other hand, well, the same reason had its cons, too. Someone was bound to notice the similarities between herself and Samuel eventually. What then? She didn't have a good answer. But she did know that she needed a cash flow of some sort while she snooped around Cold Plains. The doctor's offer solved two of three problems. She'd just have to deal with the other some way.

Smiling, she thrust her hand out. "Dr. Black, you've just landed yourself a receptionist. When do I start?"

Per his conversation with Hawk Bledsoe, he'd been planning to hire the new woman in town, but he hadn't expected her to be carried into his office after fainting; he also hadn't expected her to be so pretty.

Midnight hair with striking blue eyes that shone like the ocean in sunlight, she was enough to make a lesser man drool. Rafe wasn't immune to a woman's charms, but since arriving in Cold Plains he'd kept to himself. He hadn't uprooted his life, basically going undercover in a rogue attempt to find his son, to mess around in some casual affair. And thus far, it'd been fairly easy to stay focused.

Until now.

If he hadn't already agreed to hire the woman, he would've sent her packing. She was temptation and that was the last thing he needed.

He smothered the frown starting to build when he thought of the complication this woman represented through no fault of her own. She couldn't help looking the way she did. There was something familiar about the woman that he couldn't quite put his finger on. There were bigger problems, he reminded himself and moved on. "You can start tomorrow. Does that work for you?"

"Sure," she said, following him into the lobby. "What's the pay like?"

"Decent," he answered with a shrug. "More than minimum wage."

"Sounds good to me. How about the hours?"

"The clinic is open five days a week from 8:00 a.m. to 5:00 p.m., though I have been known to stay open for certain patients. Just ask me before you book a late night and we'll play it by ear. You get an hour for lunch, and payday is every two weeks." He gave her yellow, thin, strappy sundress a quick perusal, pretending not to notice the swell of her breasts, and said, "Business-casual attire, if you wouldn't mind."

She glanced down at her cleavage and actually blushed a little. "Sorry. I didn't plan on an impromptu job interview."

Rafe hated to sound like such a prig, but there were some very conservative types in town, and he didn't want to ruffle feathers, particularly when he was putting an image of himself out there of a suitable candidate for pledging. He smiled, hoping it came across as warm and not uptight, saying, "It's okay. I understand. So, tomorrow, bright and early? Please plan to arrive fifteen minutes early to familiarize yourself with the phone system. Where are you staying?"

"Uh, the hotel for now. Know of anyone renting a room?"

"No, sorry," he said. There was no way he was going to offer the spare bedroom in his small two-bedroom cottage on the outskirts of town. For one, it was too cozy, and the idea of bumping into the woman at all hours posed too dangerous of an opportunity for slipups. "But I'll keep an eye and ear out for anyone who might be," he added, to be helpful.

"Thanks," she said, shouldering her purse, glancing around as if wondering if they were supposed to chitchat or something to break the ice when neither were sure of the protocol. "So, what's with the self-help seminars each night?"

A derisive smirk threatened but he held it in check. Samuel Grayson fancied himself some kind of guru, and there were plenty of people buying in, so until he knew that Darcy wasn't among the followers, he'd play the part. He went to a small refrigerator and pulled out a bottled water to hand to her. "Have you had a chance to try the tonic water? It's sort of Cold Plains's signature thing."

She accepted the bottle with a quizzical expression. "What's with the water?"

"According to local legend, a restorative ribbon of water flows through Cold Plains. Samuel bottles the water from a secret location and distributes it to his people. Just another proponent of healthy living."

Darcy studied the label for a moment, her expression inscrutable, and he wondered if she bought into the whole magic-water concept Samuel liked to play up, but he was left to wonder because she simply shrugged as if she was open to the possibility and asked, "So, how come there's a price here on the label? They aren't free?"

He smiled. "Nothing in life is free, even in Cold Plains. Devotees are encouraged to purchase and drink the tonic as a symbol of unity but also for good health."

"Must work. Seems Cold Plains is full of healthy people," she quipped, flashing a playful smile that showcased straight white teeth.

If only she knew the truth of just how "healthy" the population of the town really was…. Samuel abhorred illness, imperfection and unattractive people. Speaking of, Bledsoe was right about Darcy. The minute Samuel saw Darcy, he'd want to fold her into his flock—possibly even into his bed. There were rumors of Samuel cherry-picking from his flock to satisfy his sexual needs.

Darcy raised the bottle, her brow lifting. "So, what's the damage?" she asked, referencing the water.

He waved her away. "This one's on the house. But expect to shell out $25 at the next seminar."

She couldn't help her shock. "Thanks for the heads-up, but what the heck is in this tonic water? For $25 it better be the Fountain of Youth," she said, unable to understand why anyone in their right mind would pay so much for water. He didn't blame her; he agreed it was outrageous.

"It's part of the magic of Cold Plains," he answered with an enigmatic smile.

"I guess so," she said. "See you tomorrow morning, Dr. Black." She waved and let herself out.

Rafe watched her cross the street and head toward the row of shops lining the main street, possibly more sightseeing of her new adopted town. The poor girl… He couldn't imagine that she had a clue as to what she'd gotten herself into.

Hell, did anyone?

Cold Plains was the Bermuda Triangle of the Midwest. People came in…but didn't always come out.

Alive.

Chapter 5

Darcy left the doctor's office with all manner of jumbled thoughts going through her head. What kind of man hired a woman right off the street? She could be a criminal, for crying out loud. Was there no crime in Cold Plains, that everyone was so blindly trusting? Chalk that up to another item in the *weird* column. She sighed and rubbed the back of her head where she must've hit it when she fell to the floor. *Oh, how mortifying,* she thought with a grimace. She'd never fainted in her life. Hopefully, this wasn't the start of a distressing new trend. Granted, it wasn't every day she saw her birth father. Funny, she'd never given her biological father much thought. The story Louise had told her had been that he'd knocked her up and then split, not much to talk about. And Louise had always been so tight-lipped about it, she figured it was probably a painful time in her life. Of course now Darcy knew differently. That her birth father hadn't exactly split, but her mother cer-

tainly had. She blinked back sudden tears at the thought
of Louise and everything that had happened in the past
month. The grief still pulsed under the surface, but Darcy
had been ruthless with herself, too determined to find answers to give in to the pain that scalded her heart. And
now was no different. She ground the moisture from her
eyes and focused on aligning the situation with the facts
as she knew them.

What to do about Samuel Grayson? Surely if he saw her
face-to-face, he'd notice the striking similarity between
them. Or maybe not. Maybe she'd slide under his radar.
The man was probably pretty busy running the town,
pushing his tonic water. Speaking of… She twisted the cap
of the water and took a tentative sip. *Eh. Not bad.* But certainly not worth the $25 price tag, unless it truly did have
restorative properties. However, not likely. She inhaled the
sweet, clean air and then wrinkled her nose at the sharp
unfamiliar scent of blue skies and green grass of rural Wyoming. She took another drink of the tonic water. No Star-
bucks or Pete's that she could see, and she could really use
a shot of espresso to clear her mind. She spied a small cof-
feehouse sandwiched between two other shops and made
a beeline straight toward it. Cold Plains Coffee—straight
to the point, she thought wryly and stepped inside.

A sense of foreboding followed Rafe after Darcy left.
He'd told Hawk he'd hire the woman, and he had against
his better judgment, but something else gnawed at him that
he couldn't quite place. And it wasn't just that she was a
beautiful woman. If he couldn't handle himself around a
woman who had a great body and a face to match, he had
bigger problems because Cold Plains was full of attractive
women. It was something else…. His gut told him she was

trouble. He scrubbed his palms across his face and pushed Darcy from his mind.

He pulled his BlackBerry from his pocket and opened a file he kept in a cloud network that he could access from his phone. He didn't trust an actual computer to keep his notes because computers could be breached. All the cloud network required was a smartphone with Wi-Fi connectivity, and he was good. He tapped in Darcy's name and his initial impression of the woman: pretty—might be trouble. Hired as receptionist at clinic. Unknown if she's a Devotee.

Rafe logged off and pocketed his BlackBerry, which he kept with him at all times. He used the excuse that his clinic phone would forward to his cell during off-hours, but that was just a ruse to keep Samuel off his tail. Keeping Samuel thinking that he was playing for the home team enabled Rafe to slip in and out of places he would've been barred from otherwise.

Unfortunately, the one place he hadn't been able to gain access was the one place he needed to go—Samuel's secret medical infirmary.

If there was one. That was the question he couldn't seem to find an answer to. No one was willing to admit that certain patients never returned from a visit to the clinic.

He suddenly thought of Liza Burbage as an example, an older woman suffering from type 2 diabetes who'd ignored multiple attempts to get her to change her diet so her diabetes wouldn't change from type 2 to insulin-dependent. He still remembered the conversation he'd had with her after Samuel had approached him regarding her health.

"Liza, you really need to start watching your diet. No more cookies or sweets. Vegetables and lean protein," he'd said, troubled by her recent weight gain and instable insulin numbers. "The Glucophage at the current dosage isn't working any longer to control your insulin. We're going to increase the dosage, but after that, we're out of options."

Liza sighed, a sound heavy with self-condemnation, and said, "I know, Dr. Black. I'm trying. It's just so hard. I crave sweets and carbs."

"Did you go to the clinic nutritionist?" he asked.

She made a face. "That sour-faced stick woman? She wanted me to cut my calories so much, I'd likely starve. And she wanted me to do weekly weigh-ins and sign a document that said I'd accept responsibility for increased weight while on the program. I don't know, but it just felt so regimented. I'm more of a free-spirited kind of person. You know? And I like a cookie now and then." She offered a shy but sweetly dimpled smile and shrugged. "Oh well, it's my health and my problem. Last I checked, being overweight wasn't a crime," she said with a laugh.

Rafe nodded, but a frown threatened over something Samuel had made mention of when Samuel had come to him regarding the implementation of a Devotee meal plan. Of course Rafe had offered suggestions but, in the end, admitted nutrition as a science wasn't his forte, which was when Samuel had brought in Heidi Kruch. And Rafe agreed with Liza—the nutritionist was a bit of a Nazi when it came to calorie counting. But Samuel found her approach in line with his personal philosophy, so she became the clinic nutritionist and Rafe was encouraged to send anyone with weight issues to pay a visit to Heidi to "get with the program."

To date, Liza hadn't gotten the message and not only was her weight ballooning, but her insulin levels were reaching dangerous levels. Rafe didn't care if his patients were pleasantly plump as long their health wasn't an issue. However, Samuel believed everyone ought to treat their body as a temple, and he aimed to see that everyone in Cold Plains was fit, healthy and happy. There were work-out requirements, meal plans, tonic-water intake charts, morning yoga meetings and countless other measures aimed at creating exactly what Samuel was going for: cookie-cutter people.

"Please consider giving Heidi another chance," he'd said, hating the words coming from his mouth. "She's good at putting together meal plans that will improve your insulin numbers and ultimately your overall health." He felt as if he were reading from a script, and he had no in-terest in playing the part. When Liza's expression turned dour, he said, "I know she's not the most personable, but don't throw the baby out with the bathwater. The patients who have followed her advice have been successful in losing weight and improving their overall health."

Liza sighed. "I'll think about it, but only because you're so nice about it, Dr. Black. Too bad you weren't the nutri-tionist. I'd listen to what you have to say simply because you're so cute."

"Ahh." He chuckled, yet inside he was twisting with his conscience. Liza was the wrong candidate for a nutrition-ist at this stage in her food addiction. She needed more than charts and strict rules. Likely, she needed counsel-ing to determine why she self-sabotaged with food even when her health was at stake. But Samuel didn't like head docs, as he called them. No small wonder there, seeing as a psychiatrist might question the mind-scramble Samuel did daily on the local people of Cold Plains. "Well, I hope you change your mind."

He saw Liza out after she promised to check in with

him in two weeks to do another insulin check. She never came back.

Considering their personable patient-doctor relationship and her distate for Heidi, the nutritionist, he found her absence suspect and it only provided fuel for his suspicion that Samuel made people go away if they didn't "get with the program." But for now he put it out of his mind.

Rafe spent the last few hours of the day tending to patients with various ailments—nothing more serious than the occasional flu bout or allergy flare-up—and when he flipped his sign and shut down his office, he wondered where Darcy was and what she was doing. The town wasn't large, and there was little in the way of entertainment available that wasn't sanctioned by Samuel. There was line dancing and ballroom dancing, knitting and quilting and creative brainstorming (a class Samuel suggested everyone take at least a few times a month to help with the marketing of the Cold Plains tonic water) but nothing like a dance club or bar that supported a wild time. He didn't know Darcy, but he sensed she was a city girl, accustomed to everything a city had to offer.

He was tempted to casually stroll the main street to see if she was in any of the small shops, doing the tourist thing, but as he shut the lights and started to head that direction, he stopped. What was he doing? He didn't care what she was doing or if she was bored out of her mind in the small town. Doing an abrupt about-face, he went to his car and climbed in.

He lived a short drive from town, but he appreciated the distance. Sometimes, playing the dutiful doctor wore on his nerves, and by the end of the day, he wanted to throw the mask across the room.

But it seemed relaxation wasn't in his future tonight

because parked in his short driveway was Police Chief Bo Fargo's cruiser.

Rafe muttered a curse word but pasted a smile on for Fargo's benefit.

"Evening, Chief. What can I do for you?" he asked, not commenting on the odd fact that the older man was making a house call when he easily could've stopped by the clinic if he'd wanted to chat.

Bo Fargo was a big man with a belly that protruded over his utility belt, and hard eyes that never seemed to smile. Rafe had heard stories that Fargo was a bully and that when he couldn't get what he wanted with the strength of his authority, he used his meaty, ham-hock fists. But in spite of Fargo's character flaws, Rafe couldn't be sure if he was a Devotee or not. The man didn't follow the meal plan, plainly didn't exercise and didn't seem particularly enamored with anyone, much less Samuel Grayson, so that made him difficult to categorize in Rafe's book. He hadn't mentioned to Fargo about his missing baby, but with each brick wall and dead end, he wondered if it wasn't time to elicit the help of law enforcement. To Rafe's knowledge, that jack wad outside of Laramie hadn't placed a call to Fargo like he'd said he would, but after landing in Cold Plains, Rafe realized that was probably a blessing in disguise.

Fargo acknowledged Rafe with a nod, then spit a sunflower seed shell onto the ground. "Evening, Doc. Got a minute?" he asked, the question plainly rhetorical, and they both knew it. Still Rafe smiled, as if being harassed by the local cop wasn't an inconvenience at all, and leaned casually against his car.

"Sure. What's up?" he asked, purposefully omitting an invitation to go into the house. It was his perverse way of keeping Cold Plains on the outside and, hopefully, the craziness out of his personal sanctuary. "Something wrong? That ulcer giving you trouble again?" he asked, referencing a recent diagnosis and course of treatment that Fargo had plainly ignored.

"Ain't no ulcer. I'm fine," he muttered, plainly irritated that Rafe had mentioned it. He narrowed his stare at Rafe, as if sizing him up and finding him worthy of a second, deeper look, and said, "Word around town is that you're asking about some secret infirmary. That true? And if so, where the hell would some secret facility be hidden in a town as small as Cold Plains?"

"Secret infirmary?" Rafe maintained his neutral expression, but inside, his gut twisted in warning. Fargo seemed a fair bit puzzled by his own question and the fact that he'd had to ask it. To be fair, it wasn't a normal thing to ask. But then Cold Plains wasn't normal. He crossed his arms and seemed to be thinking about the question. When he'd done a fair search of his memory, he flat-out lied with a rueful chuckle. "Can't say that I have. But if we do have one, maybe I ought to find out if they're hiring. Private practice is murder on the insurance," he said playfully.

But Fargo wasn't laughing. Hell, Rafe wasn't sure the man knew how to laugh. "Of course there's no secret infirmary," he returned roughly, glancing away. Rafe bit his tongue to keep from calling him a liar. He'd heard enough whispers, enough hushed talk to know something was out there. "But I want to know why someone would say that you're asking about one when that's plain crazy talk."

"I agree. I'd like to know who's been saying that, because I can't remember ever asking it or even hearing about one."

Fargo grunted and adjusted his girth. "Good, because

you know Samuel doesn't like rumors like that getting spread around. It erodes community spirit. Cold Plains is a good place to live. You know that or else you wouldn't have moved here, right?"

"Of course," he said, a trickle of unease sliding down his back like a rivulet of sweat on a hot day. "Cold Plains is unlike any other place I've ever lived, and I like it here."

Satisfied, at least for the moment, Fargo climbed into his cruiser. His elbow out the window, Fargo said, "If you hear of anyone else spreading those kinds of poisonous rumors about our town, you let me know, you hear?"

"You got it, Chief," he agreed, giving the impression he shared the chief's concern. "If there's anything else you need, don't hesitate to stop by my office." *And stop making house calls, you bloated bully.* Rafe smiled for emphasis. Fargo grunted and pulled out of the driveway and then out onto the highway.

It wasn't until Fargo was gone and out of sight that Rafe breathed a little easier. That was close. He'd been sloppy, asking around about the infirmary to too many people who were apparently loyal to Samuel and his cronies. He'd have to be more careful.

Or else he might find himself at the business end of Fargo's gun.

Because Cold Plains was a nice town.

And Samuel aimed to make sure no one believed otherwise.

Chapter 6

Bo Fargo walked into Samuel's office, his thoughts still on the doc. Rafe Black said all the right things, but Bo's gut told him the doc was hiding something. He'd have to keep an eye on the man to see if his instincts were spot-on, or if he was just being extra paranoid.

Samuel Grayson, the man behind the plan, looked up from his desk, an efficient smile on his face. "How was your visit with Dr. Black?" he asked conversationally, steepling his fingers as he awaited Bo's answer. The thing about Samuel was that he seemed soft and nice, but the man was meaner than a junkyard dog when riled. Bo found the contradiction a little disconcerting. He preferred that people act one way or another, not both in a sneaky way. But no one told Samuel how to act or be, not even Bo. "I trust he was cooperative?" Samuel asked.

"Yes," Bo answered, vacillating on whether or not to share his misgivings about the doc. For whatever reasons, Samuel seemed to like Dr. Black, and Bo didn't like the idea of being the bearer of bad news. However, one thing Samuel didn't abide and that was being in the dark, and since he counted on Bo to keep him apprised of the goings-on, he decided to spill. "He said all the right things, but I don't trust that man. What do we know about him? Not much. I think he's hiding something."

"Such as?"

Bo shrugged. "Dunno. Just something in my gut that says he ain't being truthful about everything."

"Interesting." Samuel pursed his lips in thought. "What was his reaction when you asked him about the infirmary?"

"Cool as a cucumber. He denied asking about one and even made some jokes."

"It would seem a man intent on finding something would be more surprised at being questioned. How reliable was your source of information?"

Bo thought of the woman, a woman who had reportedly been turned down by the good doc for a date, and he realized the information might be unreliable, and he shared as such. "Seems the doc isn't so much into dating. The woman who told me, word has it she'd been rejected in the romance department by the doctor."

Samuel chuckled softly. "Hell hath no fury like a woman scorned, right?"

"So they say," Bo muttered. Women served two purposes in Bo's life: food and sex. And sometimes he preferred the food. He cleared his throat. "What now?"

"Rafe Black is, by all accounts, a good man. He's smart, responsible, yet keeps his head down. I like that in a Devotee. Work harder at bringing him into the flock. We could benefit from a man such as himself being on our side. And who knows? Maybe if he proves worthy, he will find himself working behind the curtain, in the infirmary. But until then, watch him. Carefully."

"You got it, boss," Bo said dutifully, his belly starting to growl, signaling the dinner hour more efficiently than any clock. "Anything else?"

"Yes, actually, there is." Samuel's expression lost its easy benign softness, that air that he was just a good-natured man out to better his slice of the world. Here was that duality that Bo found unsettling. Now Samuel looked hungry and ruthless. "I've tired of my present company. I want someone fresh—young, preferably, but not too young, of course—mid-twenties with a trim figure and nice big breasts. That's important, Bo. The breasts must be natural, none of that fake silicone garbage. When I squeeze a woman's breast, I want to feel the flesh give in my hand. Am I clear?"

"Of course," Bo said, hating these particular assignments. There was something unnatural about handpicking another man's bed partner. But he did as he was told because he liked his life. It was easy and people respected him. Sure, it was out of fear, but Bo didn't care. The women spread their legs for him when he wished and didn't care to stick around longer than they were welcome, and he appreciated that most. One last thought… "Brunette or blonde?"

Samuel spread his hands in a generous gesture. "No preference. Surprise me."

Darcy stepped into the bright morning sunlight and headed for her first day of work. She really didn't have a clue as to what being a receptionist entailed, but how hard could it be answering a few phone calls for a small

Podunk, Wyoming, doctor's office? She took a quick minute to adjust her skirt and blouse and then walked into the cozy cottage with an engaging smile directed toward Dr. Black—Rafe, what a sexy name—she wanted to make friends, didn't she? But when her smile was met with a subtle flash of a frown, she hid the disappointment by settling behind the desk with the studious intent of learning the ropes. "So, here I am bright and early. What are my job duties exactly?"

Without so much as a hello, good morning, Rafe started in. "My first patient will arrive at eight-thirty, followed by another every forty-five minutes. Try to space the patients in such a manner, but if there seems to be an emergency, go ahead and book them, and I will make time. Also, anyone who has weight issues will be directed to the town nutritionist, Heidi Kruch. Here are her business cards, in case anyone asks."

"That sounds kind of personal," she murmured, checking the card information. "Why would a doctor's office recommend any one nutritionist? That seems like a decision best left to the patient."

His brief smile was patronizing. "This is Cold Plains. Not your ordinary run-of-the-mill town. But I think you already know that, right?"

"Yeah, I think I'm getting an idea," she said, pocketing a card. She wanted to see what this nutritionist was like. "Anything else?"

"Yes. We also have pamphlets on the suggested daily workout and the menu planner if anyone needs them."

"Damn...." she exclaimed under her breath, almost without thought, at how controlled the people of Cold Plains were, down to what they put in their mouths and how many crunches they did, and immediately knew she should've kept her reaction to herself when Rafe frowned in disapproval.

"Please, no cursing. Samuel isn't a fan, and it reflects poorly on the practice now that you're the friendly face behind the desk."

She bit her lip and nodded, strangely chastised. Louise had always been trying to get her to curb her tongue but sometimes a well-timed F-bomb was exactly what the situation warranted, such as when you got cut off in traffic or the ATM machine chewed up your card and swallowed it for a late-afternoon snack. But she supposed the doctor had a point; she'd really have to watch her mouth if she wanted to fit in. She couldn't exactly get information if she was found to be undesirable company. "Sorry," she said, offering a contrite smile. "No more potty mouth. It's a bad habit I've been trying to kick," she admitted. Louise was probably crowing up in heaven, happy to know that Darcy had finally found a reason to keep the profanities at bay.

"Good." There was a slight pause, then he asked, "Where did you say you were from?"

Darcy smiled at the curiosity in his voice. "I didn't."

As if realizing he'd somehow poked his nose where it didn't belong, he apologized. "It's none of my business," he said stiffly. "I shouldn't have asked."

"No, it's okay," she rushed to assure him. Was he always going to be this rigid? If so, this job might turn out to be more difficult than she imagined. She needed him to trust her, and it didn't seem they were off to a good start. She tried again to disarm him with the power of a smile, albeit rueful this time. "I was just kidding around. Sorry. My mom always said I have an odd sense of humor. I'm from Sacramento," she lied, not wanting to share too much personal information until she knew who—if anyone—she could trust. "Big-city girl. This is a huge change for me, but I like it. Changing things up is good. Sometimes you get in a rut." She was rambling a bunch of nonsense for Rafe's benefit, but he seemed to buy it. She drew a deep breath and glanced at the clock. "Oh, almost time to open. Why don't you show me the phone system and computer setup so I don't have to bug you too much with patients."

Rafe regarded her with those dark eyes, and she immediately felt as if he was trying to determine whether or not she was being truthful. She refused the urge to squirm in her chair, knowing it would only make her look suspect, but she wondered just how close Rafe was to Samuel. For a wild moment, she hoped he wasn't, because then she could, maybe, let down her guard with him. With that shock of dark hair and equally dark eyes, Rafe was worth a second glance, and in fact, she'd be a liar if she didn't admit that when she first locked eyes with him from across the room at the community center her heart rate had kicked up a bit, but the last thing she needed was to start messing around with someone in this town. She risked a short glance from under her lashes and couldn't help it when her gaze dropped to his ring finger. No ring. Well, at least she wouldn't have to contend with a Mrs. Rafe Black popping in unannounced to check out the new employee. But how could a good-looking man like Rafe remain single in a small town filled with pretty people? Was there something beyond that classically masculine-cut jawline that gave his profile a certain outlaw charm in spite of his completely buttoned-down persona that turned people off? With a face and body like his, whatever lurked beneath the surface would have to be pretty bad indeed to get a woman to steer clear. What difference did it make? He could be Adonis for all she cared. She'd come for answers, not romance. She could count only on herself. She was alone in this world. To her horror, tears pricked her eyes and she turned abruptly so Rafe wouldn't see. "Great. I think I can handle this," she said, straightening the pencils and pens just so, giving the impression that she was the kind of person who cared if the pens and pencils were all facing the same direction when, in fact, most times she left them strewn in odd places because she never returned things where they belonged. Yet another of Louise's little nags that she'd never really listened to or noticed until she was gone.

If Rafe caught the sudden pitch to her tone, betraying her secret heartache, he didn't comment, which was a good thing because the first patient had walked through the door.

Darcy put forth her best congenial smile and focused on winning over Cold Plains, one patient at a time.

Someone in this town had answers to what had happened to her mother.

And nothing was going to get in her way of finding out.

Chapter 7

In hindsight, Rafe probably should've given Darcy a better heads-up on what it was like to be his receptionist. By the end of the day, she looked frazzled and a bit dazed. His plan had been to politely follow her out the door and go his separate way, but his conscience pricked him into offering to take her to get a bite.

"You don't have to do that," she said, eyeing him warily, trying to ascertain his motivation.

He didn't blame her. He was her boss, and how was she to know that he wasn't the sleazy type who chased skirts from the office? He tried a smile—nothing flirty or suggestive, simply kind—and said, "You're new in town and you probably met just about everyone from Cold Plains in the space of an eight-hour day, but you look a bit worn around the edges. I should've warned you that my office gets a fair amount of traffic. Dinner is the least I can do for throwing you to the wolves like that. For what it's worth, you did a good job for your first day."

A smile threatened and he ignored the tickle of attraction that fluttered to life. The smile that had flirted with her mouth appeared as she said, "Well, don't go crazy with the praise just yet. I think I may have accidentally hung up on at least three patients."

He waved away her admission. "If it was important, they'd have called back or just marched into the office. I'm sure it's fine. So, how about that bite?"

"I don't know," she said. "It doesn't seem right, you know? Small towns are notorious for gossip, and I don't mean to start rumors myself, but I got the distinct impression a few of your patients were trying to play matchmaker."

"Oh?"

"Yeah, they asked if I was single and when I said I was, they quickly mentioned that you were single, as well."

Rafe smothered a sigh. Samuel fancied himself a matchmaker and openly encouraged marriage and family ties. Samuel said it was because strong families were the backbone to any successful community. Rafe was a bit more cynical. He believed Samuel pushed the family angle because a single person had less to lose. If needed, loved ones provided excellent leverage.

"Let me just say this now. I'm not looking for a date or a good time. My life is my work. I don't have time for casual or serious romantic encounters. You can rest easy. I'm not trying to butter you up for anything other than friendship."

"I appreciate your candor," she said, adding with a slight frown, "I think. But since I am new here and I certainly don't want to color anyone's opinion of me right from the start, I'm just going to go back to the hotel and order a pizza or something."

He made a sound, and she looked at him in question. "No take-out pizza places here. I think you can get a variation of a pizza at Cold Plains Italian, but I think it's a bit pricey for what you're looking for. If you're looking for a quick bite, there's the Cold Plains Eatery with deli sandwiches and whatnot."

"No pizza?" she murmured, frowning. "They ought to put that on the brochure for this place. So, why no pizza places? Not wholesome enough?"

He caught the subtle sarcasm. Most eager transplants to Cold Plains were delighted when they discovered how health conscious the town was and how dedicated to clean living everyone seemed. Darcy didn't appear the average Cold Plains transplant in search of the utopia. But if she wasn't looking for that, why would she move here? There was definitely more to the dark-haired beauty than met the eye, and in this place, that was dangerous.

As if realizing she may have revealed more about herself than she intended, she shrugged and said, "Well, that's probably a good thing. Pizza is my secret weakness. I'm better off without the temptation." She drew a deep breath and smiled. "Well, tomorrow morning comes bright and early. Good night, Dr. Black."

"Good night, Darcy," he returned, watching as she headed toward the hotel where she was staying. He didn't care what she said, there wasn't an ounce of extra fat on her body from too-much-pizza indulgence. Her tight waist flared to sweet hips, reminding him that he was a man with needs, even if he tried like hell to bury them. The last time he'd had sex was with Abby. It wasn't like he was naturally celibate, but he hadn't lied when he'd said his life was his work. Before Abby he'd concentrated on building his career. He'd been eyeing the chief of medicine position at the hospital he'd been with. After Abby had dropped her bombshell about the baby and then ended up dead, he'd been consumed with finding Devin. That left little time for personal interactions of the intimate sort. But damn, suppressing those urges would be difficult with Darcy around. There was something about her that twisted his head. Growling to himself for even thinking such thoughts, he went to his car, determined to push Darcy from his mind. She was his receptionist, nothing more.

Darcy was fairly certain she was shaking with nervous energy and not because she'd been tempted to accept Rafe's offer of dinner. She hadn't needed his assurances that he wasn't looking for an easy or convenient bed partner when he'd extended the offer—somehow she doubted he was that kind of man anyway—but just hearing the words had caused all manner of inappropriate images to crowd her brain, and her own reckless reaction was troubling. There were moments when she questioned the impetuousness of her decision to leave everything behind to go on this quest for answers, but when she found herself waffling, all she had to do was remind herself that she didn't have anyone else to watch her back, and if Samuel was dangerous, she needed to be aware of the threat. Plus, someone in this town had to know something about her birth mother. She had to believe that. Maybe she had family on her mother's side. Maybe she wasn't alone, after all. But she wouldn't know if she allowed fear to make her decisions.

After spritzing her face and dusting her lashes with

some mascara, she headed back out. She wanted to nose around, see if she could get some information about Samuel and her mother. But where to start? She didn't want to just randomly approach people and pepper them with questions. That would only make her look suspect, for sure. So how did she make it appear as if she were like everyone else in this town? Laughter drew her attention and she realized the community center—the seeming hub of the town—was alive and teeming with people.

Must be some kind of shindig going down tonight, she surmised. What better way to get involved than to jump in with both feet, right?

Absolutely.

She walked straight to the community center and filed in with everyone else.

Bo Fargo stood at the door of the community center at his usual post as people, smiling and laughing like the sheep they were, walked into the center for the nightly meeting. Bo nodded in greeting to a few but otherwise kept his expression neutral. It was no good to get too personal with these people because he never wanted to have to make a choice between loyalty to Samuel and his own feelings for someone else.

A woman—someone he didn't know—walked by, her eyes scanning the crowd without recognition, plainly a newcomer. Not bad on the eyes, she was a brunette with a nice butt and just the kind of rack Samuel preferred. Maybe his hunting expedition wouldn't be so difficult, after all. Newcomers were easy picking. They were eager to please, blinded by Samuel's charisma and charm, and usually ridiculously flattered and awestruck that Samuel wanted to spend time with them. His mouth twitched with a smile. Good. Now that he had his quarry selected, he could put a plan into action. Knowing that part of his assignment was completed, his mind wandered to his own desires. It'd been a while since he'd bedded a woman. Maybe tonight he'd find one of his regular lays, women who didn't mind spreading their legs for a little extra favor in Bo's regard, and ease up on some of the tension that seemed to ride him harder than any of the women he picked up.

Speaking of which, Brenda Billings tried to walk by without being noticed, but he snagged her arm before she could get away.

"Nice to see you, Brenda," he said, rubbing his thumb along her forearm, communicating his intent without having to spell it out for everyone to hear. She ducked her head and nodded with a slight tremble of her lip. "I haven't seen you around. Everything okay?" he asked, not truly caring, but he liked to give the appearance of a protector. "I've missed your pretty face at the meetings." The only reason he'd noted her absence was because he was horny and she was the best of his little stable of regulars. He liked the way her little body squirmed beneath the weight of his and the way she let him do unspeakably dirty things to her without complaint.

"I…I've been sick," she said, pulling her arm free with a quick glance around to see if anyone had seen their exchange. He narrowed his stare. What happened to his docile Brenda? He didn't dare draw too much attention here at the center, but he gave Brenda a look that promised a return to the subject later. "I have to get my seat," she said, moving away with a halfhearted promise, "I'll talk with you later."

"I look forward to it," he said under his breath.

Thrown off focus for a moment and his mood soured by Brenda's subtle rejection, he stalked from his post and into the hall, where he tried to find the woman he'd seen earlier.

He found her, interestingly enough, sitting not far from Brenda.

Perfect. Now he could watch them both. His mood improved, but only once he envisioned having both women service him the way he knew Samuel did with his women. Samuel could get away with that because he was handsome, charismatic and powerful. Bo knew his place in the world. The only reason women allowed him between their thighs was because he was Samuel's muscle. Without Samuel, he'd have nothing. It wasn't the way he'd imagined his life at this point in his career, but he wasn't the type to cry in his beer about what could've been. And right now, he wanted Brenda.

Whether she wanted him or not.

Darcy settled in her seat, a little bit in awe of the turnout for the nightly meeting. When she'd heard that the community met every night for some inspirational *blah blah* by Samuel, she'd expected a small contingent of people—maybe diehards—to show up. Not the whole freaking town!

Her reaction must've been noted, for the person beside her tapped her lightly and said with a friendly smile, "Amazing, isn't it?"

Startled, she swung her gaze to the woman beside her and jerked a short nod, temporarily at a loss for words or maybe just words that weren't laced with the extreme discomfort she felt by being surrounded by obvious cult members. "I had no idea there were so many...um...

devoted people," she finally said, eliciting a soft chuckle from the woman who had subsequently introduced herself as Pam Donnelly. "So, what happens at these meetings that's so special?"

"Oh honey, having a nightly meeting is just one of the many ways Mr. Grayson keeps our community strong. When you're not connected to your neighbor, it's easy to let outside influences color your thinking. Mr. Grayson is all about health and clean living, morally, financially and ethically. Even environmentally! He's a visionary, to be sure." She lifted her exorbitantly expensive tonic-water bottle. "Did you purchase a bottle?"

Flushing in embarrassment, she shook her head. "I didn't realize it was required."

"That's okay, honey. Just pick one up on the way out. Sales from the tonic water help keep our town special. Did you notice how clean our streets are? How fresh and new the playground equipment is?"

"Yes, actually, I did notice," Darcy answered, remembering how creepy it had seemed even though, admittedly, on the surface, clean streets shouldn't seem disturbing, but they were. And when coupled with everything Darcy had begun to learn about Cold Plains, it added up to *weird*. "It's great," she lied with a smile. "Cold Plains is so amazing."

Pam beamed, happy with her response. "Have you met with Mr. Grayson yet? He likes to personally greet all newcomers to Cold Plains. Oh, and you're going to love him. He's very handsome but it's more than that. He's... I don't know how to describe it. He makes you feel as if you're the most important person in the room. Heck, in the world," she gushed.

Darcy fought the urge to raise her brow. "He sounds

like a very interesting person," she said. "Maybe I'll meet him tonight. Do I have to make an appointment?"

Pam smiled coyly and said something that chilled Darcy's blood. "It's likely he already knows about you. Mr. Grayson knows everything that goes on in his town."

Darcy couldn't resist. "That doesn't seem a little… intrusive? I mean, people like a certain amount of privacy, right?"

"Well, honey, it's not like you're being spied on in the restroom." Pam chuckled. "But a close community is a connected community, that's what Mr. Grayson says. Oh, and that reminds me, did you get your health screening over at the urgent-care clinic? It's not required, but it's certainly looked upon with favor if you plan to put down roots here in town."

"A health screening?"

"Oh yes, it's very beneficial. When I had mine, I was a little overweight. Not now. Just look at me." She gestured to her figure. "No lumps or rolls any longer and I feel great. Not that you have that problem, dear. You have a lovely figure. Mr. Grayson will certainly approve."

It was the way Pam said it that made Darcy feel a little ill. Of course the woman had no way of knowing she was Samuel's daughter, but even so, something about earning Samuel's approval in any way made Darcy want to do something outlandishly reckless so there was no way he would ever approve. Maybe it was some long-buried need to rebel against the absent father figure in her life, but thankfully, self-preservation won out, and she wisely continued to smile and nod. "Well, I work for Dr. Black now, so perhaps he could do my health screening for me," she said but was surprised when Pam shook her head.

"Oh no, honey. It has to be at the clinic," she said

firmly. "Dr. Black is a nice man but he's not completely committed yet, so it's best to conduct your important business at the clinic. But don't worry, they have the best of everything there. You couldn't be in better hands. In fact, just last week I had a dark sunspot removed from my shoulder that could've turned cancerous, and I barely have a scar from the laser."

"If it wasn't cancerous, why'd you have it removed? I've heard those lasers are painful."

Pam laughed and waved away her statement. "It was so ugly. A little pain was worth getting rid of it. Besides, I wouldn't want Mr. Grayson to think I wasn't being health conscious by letting a little pain stand in my way." The lights dimmed, signaling the start of the presentation, and Pam became giddy as a schoolgirl with a crush. "Ohh, here he comes." The way Pam's eyes lit up, Darcy amended her assessment. Pam did have a crush on Samuel. Gross.

She focused on the stage, determined this time not to faint. She wanted to get a good look at the man who had fathered her.

And possibly killed her mother.

Chapter 8

Rafe purposefully grabbed a beer even though Samuel frowned on alcohol use, another passive-aggressive snub at Samuel on Rafe's part, and cracked it open with a long sigh for an equally long day. After double-checking doors and windows—he'd never been this paranoid before moving to Cold Plains—he settled into the high-backed leather chair stationed at his desk and pulled the photo of Devin from his wallet. He kept it with him, gaining a modicum of comfort having his image near, even though logically he knew it was an illusion. He didn't know if his son was alive, whether he was being cared for or whether he was being abused in some dark basement. He tried not to let his mind wander on most days, but tonight, fatigue weakened his mental walls and fear ate him.

He'd put a few careful calls out today, asking about Abby and her role in Samuel's life before she disappeared. So far, he'd gotten nothing. Sure, they remembered the woman, but no one remembered her being pregnant or if she'd been dating Samuel.

Not that Samuel dated. He selected beautiful women to "mentor," which seemed a code for screwing their brains out at his convenience. He hated to think Abby had been one of his *mentorees,* but there was a reason Abby was eliminated, and that was the only reason Rafe could think of that would've put her in danger.

But then her pregnancy would've shown at some point, and he highly doubted Samuel would've been aroused by a pregnant woman. Was her pregnancy the reason she'd incurred his wrath? For all his matchmaking and supposed, professed love for families, he was particularly averse to children and babies. Of course this was something only his closest inner circle knew, and Rafe had only discovered this fact from a seemingly innocuous statement a patient had made one day.

"You know what I like most about Samuel Grayson?" Melissa Pedersen had stated one day during a wellness check for her pregnancy. Melissa was a mother of four already, with the bun in the oven making six because she was carrying twins. "He doesn't pretend to be something he's not," she said, smoothing her hand over her large belly. "You know how politicians are always hugging and kissing kids that aren't theirs, just to give off the impression they're everyday kind of guys just like you?" Rafe nodded, curious as to where this was going. "But I think he's perfectly fine admitting babies—or pregnant women—just aren't his thing."

Rafe pretended to listen to the babies' heartbeats with his scope, but in truth, he was trained intently on what Melissa was blithely sharing. "And why do you say that?" he asked.

"Oh, because he gets this look on his face, almost like he's scared or something of a pregnant belly." She laughed as if that was either the cutest or the darndest thing, but the revelation gave Rafe chilling clarity. Melissa continued to prattle on, completely missing the sudden tension in Rafe's body. "The look on his face was one of someone afraid an alien was going to jump out at him or something. It was funny watching this confident, sexy man get so... I don't know, it wasn't that he was freaked or anything— he'd never do something so rude—but you could definitely tell, he isn't cut out to be a father. But that's okay," Melissa defended as if she'd realized someone might find what she'd said offensive. "Not everyone is cut out to do the work that he does. I imagine it takes a whole lot of concentration and time to keep a town like Cold Plains operating like a well-oiled machine, so it doesn't bother me any that he's not a family man."

Rafe had nodded and murmured assent, but his mind had turned a few cogs forward. If Abby had been Samuel's girlfriend and then gotten pregnant with another man's child, that would be sufficient enough cause to enrage Samuel.

Of course it'd been only a theory, and one he hadn't been able to prove, but he'd logged his findings in his cloud network files for future reference.

The quiet of the small house pressed on him until he couldn't stand it any longer. He wanted to go to bed, but as tired as his body was, his mind refused to shut down. He felt so helpless, so ineffectual in that he hadn't been able to find his son or find out who had killed Abby. It was times like this that he had to admit he was out of his element. He wasn't a cop, for crying out loud, yet here he was, trying his damnedest to solve a crime even the FBI was having difficulty in nailing. His chest tightened and he took a few deliberate breaths to shake loose the tension. Sometimes he wondered if that tight feeling was the need to scream his rage, grief and whatever else he had locked in there so he didn't lose it on Main Street and get carted off by one of Samuel's goons. Hell, that was probably the best way to find the infirmary, except he had an inkling that if he went down that road, he wouldn't be coming back. He took a few more swigs and then dumped the rest down the kitchen drain.

The answers he sought weren't in that bottle. He was beginning to despair that the answers weren't to be found anywhere.

He tossed the bottle into a recycle bin and shut off the lights. Maybe sleep would find him if he went to bed.

It was worth a shot—and if sleep eluded him, it certainly wouldn't be the first time he'd spent a night staring at the ceiling, anxious and afraid that Devin was long gone, no matter what he managed to shake out of Samuel Grayson.

It was starting to feel familiar.

Darcy couldn't believe how enamored the community was of her father. Maybe she was immune to his charm. She saw a man manipulating a flock of sheep to his benefit and scooping up the riches they plunked at his feet. Darcy saw beyond the fit, handsome, charismatic character who spouted platitudes that espoused loyalty and the need to be the best version of themselves by following his dictates, whether they were in the form of the menu plan or exercise regimen. Frankly, Darcy found Samuel's spiel intrusive and ridiculous. Particularly the $25 bottle of water. For all she knew, this "special tonic" could be bottled outside from a hose in Samuel's backyard.

"Isn't he amazing?" breathed Pam, in awe after Samuel had left the stage and people started to rise from their seats, the sound of laughter and gaiety filling the auditorium with a din of murmured voices. "I love these nightly meetings. They're so inspiring. Don't you agree?"

"Oh yes," Darcy said, nodding. "So, every night people do this?"

"Yes. It's about faith and loyalty. Backbones—"

"—of a strong community," Darcy finished for Pam, earning a delighted grin. "Yeah, that's what he said, so it must be true. He obviously knows what he's talking about."

"You're catching on fast. Do you want to meet him?" she asked, her eyes lighting up. "I know he'll want to meet you. Maybe if you're lucky…you might catch his eye."

Ugh. Darcy hid the immediate queasiness in her stomach. "Oh, I'm not ready to meet Mr. Grayson just yet," she protested, feigning a case of jitters as if Samuel were a celebrity and she were seeking an autograph. "Soon, though. I definitely want to meet him."

Pam sighed as if disappointed. Maybe she hoped to earn brownie points of some sort by dragging a newbie over to Samuel for inspection. The thought was sobering.

Darcy made a show of checking her watch and then said, "Oh! I'd better get my tonic water before they're sold out for the evening. So nice to meet you, Pam. I hope to see you around."

"Likewise, honey! And don't you worry, I think you're going to fit in just fine around here. You've got the Cold Plains spirit. I can tell."

Darcy forced a smile. She didn't know about that,

but there was certainly something she shared with Cold Plains…the DNA of its self-proclaimed messiah.

Edging her way past the crowd, she made a stop at the tonic-water booth, made her obligatory purchase even as she winced at the exorbitant price and wondered if Rafe was there.

Seeing nothing but a sea of unfamiliar faces, she found herself a bit relieved that she didn't see her new boss milling about with the rest of the sheep. She wanted him to be better than the rest of these people who mindlessly ate the manure that Samuel shoveled their way. She knew it wasn't a guarantee that he wasn't on the same bandwagon just because she didn't find him here, but she wanted to believe that he was different.

Rafe…the handsome doctor with a secret in his smile and a sadness to his eyes.… Darcy had to stop herself when she realized she was thinking too much about her boss. Capping her water after a quick sip, she started for the door but was waylaid by a big, burly man in uniform with hard, watery blue eyes and big meat-hook hands, which looked as if they could crush her windpipe without him breaking a sweat. For that matter, he looked the kind of person who could take a life without thinking twice.

"New to Cold Plains?" he asked, trying for a smile, but the effort only served to make him appear to be grimacing. As if realizing he wasn't a natural at the smile, he replaced it with an expression of gruff courtesy. "Police Chief Bo Fargo. Nice to meet you. If you have any questions or trouble, don't hesitate to ring my office. Mr. Grayson has charged me with keeping the peace around our nice town, and so far, everything's been working out just right."

"It's a great town," she murmured in agreement, anxious to get away from the man. The way his stare roamed her body—not in a lecherous but, rather, clinical way—gave her the willies. "Nice to meet you, Chief Fargo. Everyone has been very kind and welcoming. Thank you," she said, moving toward the door.

"Have you met Mr. Grayson yet?" he asked, knowing courtesy would prevent her from just turning and leaving as she wanted. "He takes a special interest in newcomers, particularly ones as pretty as you."

"Is that so?" she asked, playing along to see where he was going to take the conversation.

Encouraged, he nodded with a slow smirk as if she were playing right into his game. "Mr. Grayson would most definitely like to welcome you to Cold Plains. I could arrange a meeting. Would you like that?"

Darcy made a show of being flattered and even giggled a little for good measure. "Maybe another time? I want to look my best when I meet him."

"Of course," Chief Fargo said, his grin widening as if in triumph. "I'll be seeing you then."

"Yes, I'm sure you will."

She gave him her best flirty smile and slipped from the building, eager to get away from the chunky cop and his leering stare, but most important, desperate to get away before someone else tried to put her in bed with her *father*.

Chapter 9

Bo entered the dressing room off the auditorium stage and found Samuel in his usual state of dress after a meeting, which was to mean, undress. Bo wasn't a man who enjoyed the sight of another naked man, but Samuel seemed to relish putting people in his sphere of influence off-kilter, so he made no move to grab the robe that was within reaching distance. Instead, he let all his parts hang where they would and dared Bo to say something.

Sometimes Bo tired of Samuel's little head trips and wished he could call him on them, but he wisely shelved his grievances and got to the point. He'd instructed Brenda to wait for him at her place and he was eager to join her.

"I think tonight's meeting was very productive," Samuel said, eschewing the tonic water he foisted on everyone else to sip at a glass of white wine from an expensive Italian label. "What did you think?"

I think you talk too much and you're weird. "Good,"

he agreed, getting straight to the point. "There's a new-comer that might interest you. She seems to fit the criteria of what you're looking for."

At that Samuel perked up, keen interest in his eyes. "Please, share."

"She's young, in her twenties, pretty."

"And?"

"And she seems eager to meet you. Impressed by your speech tonight, I think," he added, embellishing a little before sharing the information he'd gleaned. "Her name's Darcy Craven."

"Darcy Craven," Samuel said, rolling the name on his tongue, as if testing it, before smiling. "I like it. Tell me more."

"I don't know much, just that she's got a nice figure and a pretty face. Were you looking for much else?"

Samuel sighed as if the world offered so little that he'd take what he could get, when in fact, Samuel lived like a sultan, complete with the harem of beautiful women. "No, I suppose that'll do well enough. Yes, please arrange a meeting between myself and the lovely Ms. Craven. Of course it's my honored duty to welcome all newcomers to Cold Plains."

Particularly the women, Bo added silently but nodded his understanding. "I'll see to it."

Samuel's smile was just this side of lecherous as he no doubt reveled in the heady excitement of something new to play with, a new body to discover.

The following day, a casual comment by a patient gave Rafe the in he'd been waiting for since arriving in this town.

"They just don't have enough doctors on staff at the

clinic," Mary Lou Griggs complained to Rafe as he took her pulse for a routine checkup. "I tell you, they ought to hold a job fair or something to draw attention to the clinic. I'm sure anyone would be willing to move here once they saw how great it was to raise a family and put down roots."

Rafe nodded. "So what makes you say the clinic is short staffed?"

"Well, I went for my weekly checkup with the nutritionist—have you met her yet? She's brilliant, if a little strict, but you can't argue results. I'm down two sizes. Anyway, I waited in line for an hour before anyone could draw my blood to test my glucose levels."

Rafe covered his disappointment by shrugging with a mild smile. "Well, you probably just hit them on a particularly busy day. And besides, doctors aren't the ones who would be drawing your blood. Those are lab techs."

"Oh, I know. That was just one example. But you're right, they probably need more lab techs, too. No, the real thing, no offense, Dr. Black, is that I always go to the clinic for treatment of my sciatica because they're more holistic in their approach than you. I'm not a pill person," she added, almost apologetically, as if she'd insulted Rafe somehow with her admission.

"I don't much like pills myself," he said. "But sometimes they are a necessary evil to the treatment process. However, if you've found an alternative method to ease your pain, I'm happy to hear it."

A smile bloomed on Mary Lou's face. "I'm so glad to hear that, Dr. Black. And here I thought you were so old-fashioned when it came to holistic health. I don't know where I got that idea. You know, you ought to volunteer at the clinic every now and again. A friendly face is always nice."

"Aren't there friendly faces at the clinic?" he asked playfully to mask his true motivation.

"Oh, of course," Mary Lou amended hastily, shooting him a quick look. "I just meant, well, you're so personable, I always feel like I'm visiting a friend instead of seeing a doctor. Because, you know, doctors can be a little stand-offish at times. It's that doctor-patient thing, I suppose, and the need to retain a little distance."

Rafe nodded and said, "Well, we all have different methods. But I think you're right. Volunteering at the clinic sounds like a good idea. I'm still fairly new to the community, and that seems a good way to get to know people."

"Oh yes. I think everyone goes to the clinic at some point in their lives if they live in Cold Plains. I mean, the health exam alone would put you there, right?"

He agreed. "Everyone undergoes the health exam. Even I did."

Mary Lou did a quick, flirty appraisal, which coming from the middle-aged woman nearly made Rafe shift in embarrassment, and said, "I'm sure you passed with flying colors. You're as handsome as the devil."

Rafe laughed and murmured appropriately humble remarks before steering the conversation back to her health concerns, but his mind was elsewhere. When he'd first arrived in Cold Plains, his first stop had been at the clinic to inquire whether there were any openings—and this was before he'd discovered there was rumor of a secret infirmary—but he'd been politely turned down. He figured it was because he hadn't been vetted yet in the community's eyes, but that was months ago. And now, it seemed they needed a few extra hands. Perhaps he could land some pro bono work, gain some goodwill and possibly find an opportunity to nose around places he'd been previously shut out of.

By the end of the day, he was still preoccupied with his plan of attack when Darcy stopped him as he locked up and started to head for his car. "Dr. Black…" she ventured, appearing unsure. "Can I talk to you a minute?"

He stopped, concerned. "What's wrong?"

"Nothing," she assured him, but her expression remained pensive. "Can you tell me what this health exam is all about? Last night at the meeting, I was told all newcomers have to undergo a series of tests."

"It's just a standard battery, nothing to be alarmed about," he said. "It's more of a precautionary measure."

"Precautionary against what?"

Such an innocent question, one he had no answer for without revealing his own fears and suspicions. Tread carefully, his mind whispered, but there seemed true apprehension in her eyes. "I'd like to say you don't have to do them—by law, no one can make you do anything—but if you're interested in becoming a permanent resident of Cold Plains, you'll find an easier go of it if you've been cleared by the clinic."

"Isn't that discriminatory?" she asked.

Extremely. He shrugged. "It's the Cold Plains way."

A flash of distaste rippled over her expression and made him wonder, not for the first time, where her loyalties lived.

"I could go with you," he suggested. "I have to swing by the clinic myself."

"What are you going for?" she asked.

He smirked at her seeming inquisitive nature and answered with a shrug. "I'm checking into some volunteer positions. I've heard the clinic is short staffed and I want to help."

"You're so busy with the practice. You think you'll have time to volunteer?" she asked, mildly incredulous. "Do you have something against enjoying a private life?"

A private life... Even before Abby's bombshell, he'd eschewed lazy Sundays at the lake for board meetings, operational committees and conferences sandwiched between shifts at the hospital. He couldn't remember what it felt like to let his mind rest. Now his focus had changed, but his drive hadn't. "I like to stay busy," he said. "And I like to feel needed. Helping others is a good way to remind yourself of your blessings. Someone always has it worse than you."

Darcy's expression faltered as if she'd realized her statement had smacked of selfishness, and she bit her lip. That single action, something she'd probably done a hundred times and he'd never noticed, drew his attention and held it for an inordinate slice of time. Why had she come to Cold Plains? What was the real reason? Little by little, she gave off signs and signals that she wasn't the usual newcomer, yet she professed to be enamored with the Cold Plains lifestyle.

"I don't like needles," she confessed, embarrassed. "I mean, I *really* don't like needles. As in I'm a bit phobic. Is there a time limit for these tests?" she joked.

"No, you can do them whenever you like. May I ask why you're afraid of needles?"

"Aren't you afraid of anything?"

Not finding Devin in time. Getting found out by Samuel before I get the answers I need... Yeah, he knew a thing or two about fear. "I don't particularly like birds."

She did a double take. "Birds? As in, tweet-tweet?"

He chuckled. "Yeah. Dirty menaces."

At that, she laughed, revealing a beautiful smile that knocked him back a bit. "You know, birds are everywhere," she said.

"Welcome to my life. Aren't you glad you're only afraid of needles?"

"That does put things in perspective."

"Happy to help. You didn't say why you were afraid of needles."

Her expression turned wistful. "No, I didn't." She drew a deep breath and said, "Well, I guess it's because of my mom. She recently died of cancer, and the doctors were always poking her for one reason or another. She started to run out of places where they could poke her because her veins were collapsing and her body was covered in bruises. Every time I see a needle, I get sick to my stomach. It's hard to deal with, the memories of what she went through. So I guess, if I had to pinpoint the origin, that would be it."

"I'm sorry to hear of your mother's cancer."

"Yeah," she murmured, ducking her head. "It's still kind of raw. I try not to think about it."

"Is that why you came to Cold Plains?"

"Yes," she answered without hesitation, though there was something else in her eyes, but it was gone before he could place it. She brightened. "New place. New start. I need that. You know?" She gestured to the quaint, pristine street and the overall picture-perfect quality surrounding them. "And what a place to start fresh. This is like a little slice of heaven. Clean streets and air, a community that actually cares about each other…it's just what I needed."

"That's what most people say," he agreed. "So, just let

me know if you want someone to accompany you. I'd be happy to be the person to do that."

"Thanks, Dr. Black."

Rafe knew it was wise to keep the formality between them, but it felt wrong and forced. "Please, call me Rafe," he said. "Unless you prefer Dr. Black, of course."

She seemed unsure, and he didn't blame her. Hell, the minute he offered, he wondered if he shouldn't have kept his mouth shut, but when she slowly nodded and gave him a sidewise grin as she said, "Rafe it is," he knew things between them would start to change.

He just wasn't sure whether the change was good or not.

Either way, something had just been set in motion.

He could feel it.

Darcy watched as Rafe walked in his usual hands-in-pockets yet brisk style down the sidewalk toward his parked car, and tested Rafe's name on her tongue a few times.

It was sexy, no doubt about it.

How many doctors were named Rafe? Doctors—like accountants or dentists—were given names like George, John or Tom.

Not Rafe.

Most doctors didn't look like Rafe, either, at least not in Darcy's experience.

Everything about the sexy doc was surrounded by an air of mystery. Good Lord, she found that highly attractive.

Bad. Bad. Bad.

She should've politely reminded Rafe that a certain level of formality was good for employee-boss relations.

But she liked that he'd offered.

Darcy sighed. She supposed, try as she might, fighting her own nature was a losing battle.

Before Louise died, Darcy had been a bit of a party girl. Not dangerous and recklessly so, but she'd enjoyed a good time or two.

That seemed ages ago now.

She checked her watch—it would be time for the nightly meeting soon. She had just enough time to get back to the hotel, freshen up and do some research before heading to the community center.

But even as her mind processed the mountain of new information that seemed to come at her from all angles, she had trouble keeping her thoughts wrangled on the straight and narrow. Unfortunately, that party girl was still alive and well inside of her, even if she'd been mostly subdued as of late.

And that party girl liked what she saw in Rafe Black. She liked the fact that he was a bit mysterious—possibly dangerous—and most definitely hiding something behind those dark eyes. Overall, Rafe was a package deal of off-limits-stay-off-the-grass, and even as sternly as she reminded herself to steer clear, that was the exact opposite of what Party Girl wanted to do.

The question was, how could she stay the course in her mission to find answers, without succumbing to that reckless impulse to get to know the good doc a bit better?

It was yet another dilemma placed on an already full plate—and yet another opportunity to slip up in grand fashion with potentially deadly consequences.

Chapter 10

Rafe crossed the threshold of the clinic and enjoyed the bracing rush of cold air after being in the June heat. He walked straight to the chief of medicine's office, having made an appointment to see him personally. He wasn't going to waste time with people who didn't have any power. Now that he'd operated his practice for a few months, he felt he had more to offer, that he'd proven his loyalty.

Smile firmly in place, he walked into Dr. Virgil Cruthers's roomy office and closed the door behind him when Virgil gestured for him to do so, before he took a seat across from him.

"So good of you to see me on such short notice," Rafe started, shaking the older man's hand.

Virgil Cruthers was a white-haired man with a face and body that would look quite natural in a red Santa suit, but Rafe saw past the soft wrinkles and grandfatherly demeanor to the sharp, cunning man behind the mask. He didn't doubt Cruthers was a Devotee, otherwise Samuel wouldn't have trusted Cruthers in such an important position. If anyone knew about a secret infirmary, Cruthers did—and likely oversaw the operation.

This was the man whose trust Rafe needed to earn and the one who was likely as dangerous as Samuel.

"I'm happy to meet with a colleague such as you, Rafe. You've earned yourself a bit of a reputation, son."

He arched his brow. "Oh?"

"All good, I assure you," Virgil said, smiling, actually pulling a file folder from his desk. That there was a file on Rafe didn't surprise him at all, but it did shock Rafe that Virgil was being so open about it. Rafe took that as a promising sign. "I see here you've been very helpful in referring patients to Heidi for help with their nutrition needs. Your success rate is hovering at eighty-five percent. Not bad."

"Success rate?"

Virgil closed the file and leaned back in his chair, regarding Rafe with keen eyes. "Each time a referral comes in, we determine where it came from, and then if the patient completes the program successfully, that reflects well on the person or agency that referred them."

"Eighty-five percent, huh? Glad to hear so many patients are being successful," he said, smothering the questions that begged to be asked: What happened if his patient success rate started to fall? What happened to the patients who failed? Rafe needed to know, but he wisely bided his time. "I'm happy to help."

"And Cold Plains needs people like you, Rafe," Virgil said sternly. "Smart, capable and with the program. I took a look at your numbers and you're in excellent physical shape, just the kind of example we like to set in Cold Plains. You're a perfect ambassador."

Rafe resisted the urge to shift in discomfort. He didn't want to be Cold Plains's poster boy for anything, but he recognized Virgil meant it as a compliment, so he reacted accordingly. "I appreciate that. I try to keep in shape, and the meal plan is very helpful in maintaining a healthy balance." God, help him, he was lying through his teeth but he'd long since ditched any reluctance to stretch the truth since moving here.

"So what can I do for you?" Virgil asked.

"I want to do more for the Cold Plains community," he said. "I heard that the clinic might need an extra pair of hands."

Virgil sighed and laced his fingers together. "True. Unfortunately, the budget doesn't support hiring another doctor, otherwise you'd be first on our list of desirables."

"I understand and that's why I want to volunteer."

"Volunteer?"

"I was raised to believe a life of service was the key to true happiness. I'm ready to be put to use here in my new community."

Virgil's expression split into an approving smile, which actually reached his eyes, and Rafe knew he'd said the right thing. "You were raised right, son," Virgil said with a short nod. "Too many in this world have no regard for their fellow man. That's what makes Cold Plains special, wouldn't you agree?"

"Completely. And I need to feel I'm doing my share."

"Ah, I like the way you think. It's a generous offer, for sure, but can you handle a practice and a volunteer schedule? That's a heavy load."

Rafe laughed. "Virgil, if I may be blunt, before I came

to Cold Plains I was gunning for the chief of medicine position at my old hospital. I don't have to tell you what that entails. I've long since forgotten what it's like to have spare time, and frankly, I'm more comfortable being busy."

"A man after my own heart," Virgil said, smiling. "I know how you feel. Just doesn't seem natural to sit on your hands and do nothing when you've got talents to share and lives to change. You're a good man, Rafe Black. Cold Plains is lucky to have someone of your character."

Rafe offered Virgil a sidewise grin. "I wouldn't go that far, but I do want to help. Can you use my services?"

"Of course," Virgil answered, yet there was hesitation in his voice. Rafe waited, not wanting to appear suspiciously eager. "Here's the situation…. Mr. Grayson has a personal stake in the running of this facility and all hiring of personnel and volunteers are passed by him first. What kind of relationship do you have with Mr. Grayson?"

Rafe made a point to appear nonplussed. "I think we're on good terms. Never had a negative run-in, if that's what you're asking."

"Good. Then I'll schedule a sit-down with you two, and if he gives you the green light, I'd be thrilled to have you on board. We could really use some help in the maternity ward. I know you don't specialize in obstetrics, but as a volunteer, you would be working under the direction of the staff OB doctor. That sound okay with you?"

Rafe couldn't have found a more perfect fit for his purposes. He smothered the grin he felt building. "I'd be happy to fill in wherever there's a need," he offered.

He was rewarded with a big smile from Virgil. "That's an excellent attitude, son. I think you're going to be just fine around here. I'll call when Mr. Grayson has an opening. And between you and me, expect a call sooner rather than later, so please have a schedule you can commit to ready for presentation to Mr. Grayson."

Rafe stood and shook Virgil's hand again. "You bet. I'll await your call."

As Rafe left the room, he caught Virgil picking up the phone. He suspected he'd be meeting with Mr. Grayson by tomorrow.

Darcy may have embellished a little on her needle phobia. It was true each time she saw a needle she cringed inwardly because of what she'd seen her mother go through, but her reluctance to get the tests done had more to do with Samuel Grayson than some phobia. She couldn't see herself allowing anyone associated with Samuel Grayson taking her DNA, because if cross matched, half would line up with Samuel himself. She imagined that wouldn't go over very well. There'd be no hiding in plain sight after that.

She crossed to the library and slipped inside but not before attracting the attention of someone else who followed her into the building.

The library seemed a good place to start to look into the past history of Cold Plains. She figured there had to be something that drew Samuel here, and she wanted to know what it was. Maybe if she knew the why, she'd gain some insight into his personality or what drove him.

Darcy went straight to the archives where the newspapers were kept on microfiche. It took her a moment to remember how to work the archaic machine, but thankfully, her college experiences, library trolling for several professors who didn't believe in the internet, came in handy.

She went back five years, flipped through issue upon issue of small-town ordinary stuff from recitals to bake sales, but when she went back further, she stumbled upon a notable difference.

"Looking for anything in particular?" A voice beside her caused her to jump and nearly fall from the stool. An officer, blond and attractive, helped her regain her seat, a look of concern on his handsome face. "Sorry about that. I didn't mean to startle you. I'll have to watch my stealth skills," he said with a slight tilt of his mouth, which was borderline flirty. "Officer Ford McCall at your service."

Darcy smiled back, not quite sure what to think of the man. Everyone here was automatically filed away in the *sheep* column, until proven otherwise, and that included overly friendly cops who popped out of nowhere to scare the bejesus out of her. "Darcy Craven," she said, extending her hand, which he accepted with a good-natured grin. She wondered at the sudden solicitousness, hating that she couldn't trust a single soul in this town. He didn't seem much older than she, maybe by a few years, and although he was good-looking, he didn't hold a candle to Rafe, not that she needed to compare. "I'm new to Cold Plains and I'm just trying to get a feel for the town. I like to read the old archived newspapers."

"Well, you're in luck. I'm a Cold Plains native," he said.

She regarded him with new interest. "Really? Born and raised?"

"Is there any other kind?"

"No, I guess not," she allowed with a small smile. If he was from here, maybe he wasn't completely on board with all the crazy, Samuel-Grayson-groupie, fan-club stuff. "So, can you tell me why Cold Plains went from a rough-and-tumble town to the next Park City? I mean you must've seen some pretty big changes since you were a kid growing up here."

"Yeah, big changes. Mostly good," he said. "Crime is down and the streets are cleaner."

"I would imagine a crime-free town isn't good for business if you're a cop," she teased to gauge where his sense of humor landed. To her relief, he offered a chagrined chuckle.

"Yeah, well, it's not completely crime free, so there's always a need for law enforcement."

"So what kind of crime are we talking?" she asked, politely fishing.

"The usual, petty theft, vandalism, the occasional burglary."

"Hard to believe from what I've seen so far," she murmured.

"I'll take that as a compliment," he said.

"So what was Cold Plains like before...?"

"Before Samuel Grayson?" he finished for her. She nodded. He paused as if considering his answer. Then, just when she thought he might deflect her question, he answered with a definitive edge to his tone. "Different."

She wasn't sure if he meant that in a good or bad way. Before she could ask for clarification, he stopped to regard her with something akin to recognition. "I know we don't know each other, but...there's something about your eyes that seems familiar.... Crazy, I know."

Darcy froze the smile on her face. He'd noticed the similarity between her features and Samuel's. She cocked her head to the side and gave a little shrug. "Hmm, my Victoria's Secret catalog isn't set to come out until Christmas.... Not sure where you might've seen me before that," she said, relieved when he laughed.

"Ah, a girl with a sense of humor. I like that. Well, I better get back to patrol or else Chief Fargo will have my hide. I couldn't resist saying hello to the newest pretty girl in town."

She swiveled to face him, her elbows resting casually on the counter. "Yeah, about that. Why is everyone here so good-looking? Hard to stand out when everyone's a looker, you know?"

"Good genes?" he supposed, then said in a conspiratorial whisper, "Well, we keep the ugly ones locked away. We're trying to build a reputation as the prettiest town in America."

She was fairly certain he was joking, but an odd chill raced down her spine just the same. "Well, I haven't been carted off for the ugly camp yet, so that must mean I passed the test."

Ford gave her an obvious once-over. "Oh yeah…you passed. With flying colors."

She actually blushed, which was odd because Darcy hadn't blushed since she was a preteen and went bra shopping with her mom and happened to run into a boy she was crushing on at the mall. It'd been completely awful, actually. Darcy had been horrified, thinking the boy had somehow known that inside that JCPenney bag was her first training bra. Of course he'd had no way of knowing, but Darcy had blushed from the roots of her scalp to the ends of her hair. "Thanks," she said, wondering if the charm he poured so easily was part of an act or who he really was as a person. "I guess I'll see you at the meeting?"

"No, I don't much like sitting still to listen to someone yammer on for an hour. Just not my thing. I'd rather be doing something."

Interesting. "Well, maybe I'll see you around."

"It's a small town. It's likely I'll run into you again

within the hour," he joked, waving as he headed for the door. "Well, welcome to Cold Plains and I'll catch you later."

She nodded and waited a minute to return to her research. Where did Officer McCall fall into the Grayson groupie files? Something told her he wasn't exactly a follower like everyone else. That alone was a point in his favor. But appearances were deceiving. She wasn't about to trust anyone on first impressions alone. Maybe she'd casually mention McCall's visit to Rafe, see what his reaction was.

Darcy lowered her head and focused on the newsprint, reading how at one time Cold Plains had been like any other small, economically depressed town, with more bars than churches and definitely less of the upwardly mobile set. A shot of downtown showed old junkers parked on the side instead of the high-end models zipping around today.

Yeah…a lot had changed. On the surface, it seemed like nothing but positive changes had been made, but at what cost? There was something weird about a town filled with pretty people. It just wasn't right.

And she knew it had to do with Samuel Grayson. The question was…what did it have to do with her mother?

Ford McCall lost the easygoing smile the minute he was clear of the woman's vision. Something about her begged another look—and it had nothing to do with her pretty face. She seemed familiar, and he couldn't quite put his finger on why. Ford hated the unknown. There was too much weird stuff going on in his hometown to discount any gut feeling.

His private cell went off and he checked the caller ID. FBI agent Hawk Bledsoe. He switched off the radio in his

Escalade, so he didn't inadvertently broadcast his conversation over the airwaves, and answered.

"McCall here."

"Agent Bledsoe."

"What's up?" he asked, scanning the street as he pulled away from Main and toward the station.

"Just checking in. Any leads on the Johanna Tate case?" he asked.

Johanna Tate—Samuel Grayson's main girlfriend up until she was found dead two months ago, eighty miles away outside Eden—was a case Ford couldn't let go of, in spite of his boss's less-than-supportive stance on the subject.

"No," he answered darkly, hating that justice was being thwarted. "Nothing so far, especially when I've got Fargo blocking me at every turn. He doesn't want me poking around, which tells me that's exactly why I need to keep at it. Anything from the lab?"

The forensic evidence from beneath Johanna's nails had been sent for testing to the FBI lab. They had far more resources, and if anything was going to show up, the FBI labs would find it.

"Not yet. These things move slow," Hawk said. "Everyone knows Johanna was Samuel's girl. There has to be someone who knows what happened to her. Keep asking around."

"Why won't you let me put some pressure on Samuel himself? He seems the most logical suspect," Ford groused. "We need to lean on him, let him know that he's not untouchable."

"Not yet," Hawk warned, pissing off Ford even more. He felt collared and neutered, tiptoeing around Samuel Grayson just because the FBI wanted to nail him with a bigger case than one murder. "Just keep doing what you're doing. Besides, you start poking at Grayson and you'll end up with a bullet sandwich for breakfast. Trust me in this. We'll get him, but we have to do it right. We've only got one shot. We can't blow it going off half-cocked just because we're itching to nail the guy. Promise me you'll keep a low profile."

"Yeah," Ford grumbled, pulling into the station. "I'm at the station. I'll check in if I hear anything new."

"Good man," Hawk said and clicked off.

Ford returned the radio to its preset and shut down his cruiser to stalk inside.

His boss, Police Chief Bo Fargo, looked up from his desk with a scowl. Fresh scratches marred his face, which only made the ornery cuss uglier. He was probably the only unattractive man allowed in Grayson's little cluster of goons. Ford wondered at the scratches but didn't care enough to ask, not that Fargo would've shared; the boss wasn't exactly a touchy-feely, hug-your-neighbor type of guy.

"Where you been?" Fargo barked. "Couldn't raise you on the radio."

"On patrol," he answered, going straight to his desk. "Radio got switched off by accident. It was only off for a minute, though."

"That seems to happen a lot," Fargo said, narrowing his gaze. "Got a problem with your equipment?"

"No, sir. Just an accident."

"See that you get a handle on it, Officer," Fargo warned.

Ford gave a curt nod and focused on his notes about Johanna Tate.

The coroner had concluded that she'd been strangled due to the ugly bruising around her larynx that was consistent with finger placement around the neck. But there were other bruises, too, that suggested a struggle, which was why Ford had made the inroads with Hawk to have the fingernail scrapings sent to the FBI lab. She'd been clothed and the sexual-assault exam had revealed no findings. And when Ford had read Fargo's report about his interview with Grayson when they'd discovered Johanna's body, Ford had been incensed at the piss-poor quality of the report.

"Grayson doesn't have an alibi," Ford had pointed out, dropping the report on Fargo's desk once Fargo had released his supplemental information. "We need to question him again. Why isn't Eden pushing this?"

Fargo had leveled his watery stare at Ford and said, "*We?* I don't recall there being a *we* on this case. *I* interviewed him and the man didn't kill his favorite girl. Eden investigators agreed. Case closed."

Ford longed to contradict his boss, but he kept his tongue in his head. "Anyone else gave us this kind of answer and we'd be digging for more information. Why not with him?"

"Samuel Grayson is a good man and he's broken up about Johanna. Have some respect, McCall. Mr. Grayson is grieving. I'm not about to hound him during his time of mourning."

Yeah, Ford could see how deeply Grayson was grieving—by screwing every woman who would lift their skirts for him. "No one says you can't be respectful in your questioning. I'd think that Grayson would want to answer our questions so we can satisfy our concerns about his involvement and move on to the next suspect. An innocent man has nothing to hide, right?"

"I cleared him. He is an innocent man."

"What about Johanna? Doesn't she deserve our full attention to her case?"

"Johanna, rest her soul, is gone. She doesn't care what happens now. The fact of the matter is, we may never know what happened to her. You know that there are millions of unsolved cases in the world. Sad but true."

"Not in Cold Plains," Ford countered with a thread of steel.

"She didn't die in Cold Plains, now, did she? My notes say she was found in Eden. That's eighty miles away. And frankly, not our case. Johanna Tate's case is Eden's responsibility, not ours. The only reason we were brought in at all was because she was a Cold Plains resident. But as far as I'm concerned, Samuel Grayson isn't a suspect and I'd better not find out that you've been harassing the man or I'll have your badge."

Ford had startled at the threat. Without ample cause, Fargo couldn't strip him of his badge, but the very fact that he'd make the threat gave Ford pause. "You're right. It's in Eden's court now," Ford conceded, adding, "which is why I suggested that the FBI take a look at the forensics. They happily agreed. Whatever was under Johanna's nails is now being tested with state-of-the-art technology. Something is bound to show up."

Fargo stilled, his stare sharpening to a razor edge. Ford held his ground. If Grayson had nothing to hide, he'd come out smelling like a rose. "My, my...you're a helpful guy, aren't you?" Fargo nearly sneered.

"Just doing my job," Ford stated evenly, refusing to let Fargo intimidate him like he bullied everyone else in this town. "I'm sure you can appreciate that, being an officer of the law yourself."

They stared each other down, a standoff of sorts, but

finally Fargo looked away first, but not before saying with a shrug, "Try to remember who you're working for, son. You could go far if you do."

"I know who I work for, Chief. The community of Cold Plains." *Not Samuel Grayson.* Finished, Ford returned to his desk, his temper spiked but under control. He had to keep a cool head, or like Hawk said, he'd be munching on lead, and his case would be filed alongside Johanna's as *unsolved.*

Chapter 11

True to his prediction, Rafe was summoned to Grayson's office to chat the following day. Rafe canceled his patient load and gave Darcy the day off, then hurried to the community center where Grayson held court.

Rafe had been introduced to Samuel when he first arrived in town, as Samuel liked to personally greet anyone who was looking to become a permanent part of his community, but the meeting had hardly been memorable, at least on Samuel's part.

Now Rafe could see keen interest light up Samuel's eyes as he entered the office. He was probably wondering, was this a man who could benefit me somehow? Another doctor in his pocket would likely serve him well. Playing the game sickened Rafe, but he was willing to do whatever he had to to find his son.

"Please, take a seat," Grayson said, gesturing to the seat opposite his expansive mahogany desk. Two tonic waters appeared, thanks to the helpful—and pretty—personal assistants Grayson kept flitting about for his business. And other things, he'd heard rumored. Rafe accepted a water and cracked it with a dutiful swig. Grayson left his untouched but appeared pleased by Rafe's actions. "I hear you want to help at the clinic? Virgil says you come highly qualified."

"Thank you, sir," Rafe said. "I'm honored that you would even consider me for service. I feel the need to do more for my community and I heard that the clinic is short staffed at the moment."

"Happily, our population continues to grow with like-minded people, but that does put a strain on our resources at present," Grayson admitted. "Our maternity ward is quite full at all times. Cold Plains is a place for families and we're overjoyed at the fertile bounty. However, more hands would be a blessing."

"Obstetrics and pediatrics aren't exactly my forte, but I'd be happy to fill in wherever I'm needed."

"Virgil said you had a good attitude. I see he was right. Tell me, have you become a Devotee to the Cold Plains way?" Grayson asked, putting Rafe on the spot.

Technically, he hadn't pledged yet and this was likely something Grayson already knew but it all hinged on how he answered. Rafe went with a variation of the truth. "I support everything Cold Plains stands for, and I attend the meetings as I can. But I haven't pledged just yet."

"Any particular reason? What's holding you back?" Grayson asked mildly as if he were merely curious, when in fact, Rafe knew he was being tested.

"Can I share a personal philosophy?" he said, sidestepping the question a little, to which Grayson nodded with curiosity. "There are people who get baptized and then do all manner of ungodly things because they think, well, hell, I'm in the clear because I've been forgiven. And then there are the people who never step foot in a church but are known by their good work. I'm a man of action, not words. I believe in the Cold Plains way. I think you've created a good thing here, but I don't feel it'd be right for me to pledge just for the sake of doing it. Know me by my actions, not my words."

Rafe held his breath, knowing he may have just shot himself in the foot. And the longer the pause went on, Rafe wished he'd just lied and said he was planning to pledge that week. But just when the tension grew to an unbearable level, Grayson broke into an amused grin, saying, "I like you. You're honest. And we need honest men." He straightened, getting to business. "But good character aside, when people pledge and become Devotees, it's more about fostering community and becoming a stronger unit by encouraging conformity to the way we live."

"Are you saying I need to pledge to volunteer at the clinic?" Rafe asked.

Grayson shrugged. "Of course not. You've proven yourself an honorable and valuable member of the community, but I'd like you to reconsider. You'd make an excellent ambassador. We need people like you on our side, promoting the Cold Plains lifestyle."

"I'll give it serious consideration," Rafe said.

"See that you do," Grayson said, looking up when an assistant appeared at the door.

"Your next appointment is here, Mr. Grayson," the pert blonde said with an adoring smile.

"Thank you, Penny," Grayson said. There was nothing in his voice to suggest impropriety, but maybe it was because Rafe had heard stories to the contrary that he couldn't help but see Grayson's gaze alight on the young woman's supple and trim curves. Penny disappeared and Grayson returned his attention to Rafe, who had already stood to take his leave. "I like that you're a straight shooter, Rafe Black. An honest man is a rarity these days. Virgil will be in touch. Thank you for coming in."

"My pleasure, Mr. Grayson," he murmured, accepting another perfunctory handshake before letting himself out. Before he walked out the front doors, he saw Penny slip into the office and heard the muffled click of the lock turning.

Disgusted, Rafe hurried from the building before he lost his lunch and blew the carefully cultivated act he'd orchestrated to dupe Grayson.

It was worth it, he reminded himself.

Anything was worth finding Devin.

Darcy caught wind of the fact that Rafe was interviewing for a volunteer position at the clinic. When they returned to the office the next day, she was full of questions that were probably none of her business, but it troubled her more than she wanted to admit, thinking that Rafe was on board with the Cold Plains cuckoos. She'd since discovered that the clinic was ground zero for the cultie sect.

"How was your meeting?" she asked, trying for nonchalant but likely failing. She'd never been much of an actress, but she supposed she'd better get skilled fast if she wanted to get anywhere here. Well, she'd get some practice with Rafe. "Everything go okay?"

"It went very well," he answered with a smile. "Did you enjoy your day off?"

Ah, polite banter. That's right. Cue the banal details of an otherwise uneventful day. "I went to the library, checked out a book or two—okay, twist my arm, it was three—and I met Officer McCall. Nice guy. Cute, too." Now, why'd she add that? Maybe to gauge Rafe's reaction.

At McCall's name, Rafe looked at her sharply. "Oh? You like him?"

"He seems nice enough. I guess he's a native. Born and raised right here in Cold Plains. Of course he said it used to be a lot different back in the day. In fact, things really started to change—for the better, of course—when Mr. Grayson decided to put down roots."

"Yes, I've heard the town was much different before Samuel…even the street names."

"Excuse me?"

"Oh yeah. You know, this used to be Oak and Elm, now it's Success Avenue and Principle Lane."

"Boy, that kinda sucks for the locals who grew up with the streets the old way," she murmured, flabbergasted that someone would move into town and then change the street names.

He shrugged. "No one seemed to complain too loudly."

They were probably afraid to, thought Darcy. "So, you're thinking of volunteering at the clinic? You're already pretty busy."

"It's important to me," he said.

"Why?" she asked.

"I…" he started, then frowned as if he'd been about to give away more than he was ready to impart. He finished with a smile. "It just is."

"I get it, something personal. I'm sorry to have pressed. I just thought that the clinic might not be your style." *As in, I'd hoped you weren't part of that group but apparently you are.* She worked hard to conceal the sharp disappointment welling in her chest. "Well, I hope you find what you're looking for."

His stare narrowed and she wondered what she'd said wrong, but whatever it was disappeared in the next blink. "My first patient will be here soon. I need to go over my case notes," he said, turning and disappearing into his office.

Darcy let out a shaky breath, wondering what sort of nerve she'd hit with her innocent comment. She'd give anything to have a peek inside that brain of his. There was a reason he pushed himself to the extreme and was now looking to volunteer at the clinic. Something didn't add up—the looks, the quiet steel behind his eyes and now this sudden urge to spend every waking moment with the community of Cold Plains. If she didn't know better, she'd say Rafe Black had something to hide, or maybe, he was looking for something, just like her.

She needed to spend more time with Rafe. But if he planned to spread himself so thin, how was she to carve any time out for her?

Leaning back in her chair, she fiddled with her bracelet, hoping inspiration would hit her. She needed a plan, something to put her closer to the man. The door opening interrupted her thoughts as Rafe's first patient entered. Shelving her personal dilemma for the moment, she put on a smile and did her best to charm everyone who walked through the front door.

Bo had received a summons from Grayson five minutes before he was set to head home. He'd grumbled when he'd read the caller ID on his phone, but he hadn't dared ignore the call, which was why, instead of enjoying a beer, he was listening to Grayson chastise him for being late with his delivery.

"What's the delay?" Grayson demanded, his patience growing thinner by each failed attempt to get Darcy Craven into Grayson's office for a "meeting."

"I can't seem to catch her. She's working a lot with Doc Black, and each time I've gone by her hotel room, she's been out."

"I'm starting to feel as if she isn't interested in meeting me."

"I'm sure that's not it," Bo assured Grayson, though it smacked of all kinds of wrong to be mollifying a grown man like a spoiled child, but in some ways, Bo had discovered Grayson could give kids a run for their money in the petulant department. "She's just new to town and getting to know people, I guess. She'll come around eventually."

"I want to meet her now," Grayson said, a dark thread weaving its way into his voice. "This is getting ridiculous."

Looking to distract Grayson, Bo said, "What happened to Penny? Your new assistant...she seemed like a nice gal."

"For a time. Speaking of, she'll need some aftercare. Take her to the clinic tomorrow. Use the back entrance. I don't need that officer of yours asking questions."

Ah hell. That meant Penny was probably a mess. Sometimes Grayson got a little overzealous in his bed play, and cuts and bruises occurred.

"Where is she?" Bo asked.

Grayson gestured to the bedroom cleverly concealed behind a false wall in his office.

"Maybe I ought to take a look."

"Be my guest. She's finally stopped crying. It wasn't even that vigorous. I hardly used the cat-o'-nine-tails."

Bo winced. The cat-o'-nine was a vicious whip. He wouldn't want that sucker striking on his butt, that was for sure. He pushed on the false wall and it swung open, revealing a young woman lying facedown on the bed, bloody welts and gashes lacing her exposed flesh. Bo rolled her over and bit back a few curses when he saw her fat lip and black eye. "Was that really necessary?" he asked, irritated at the mess he'd have to clean up.

Grayson considered the question as if it hadn't been rhetorical, then shrugged. He either didn't have an answer or didn't care to offer one. It didn't matter. Bo would be the one cleaning up his dirty work. "She needs a doctor now," he said, eyeing the unconscious girl with a critical eye. "If we wait until tomorrow, she could be dead."

"Really? I didn't think it was that serious."

"Well, it is," Bo snapped. "I'll have someone from the clinic bring a car. I can't very well load her into my cruiser, looking the way she does."

"Good thinking. Now back to the issue at hand. As you can see, I've lost my companion for the evenings. Seeing as I have an opening now with my personal assistants, perhaps we can offer Darcy a compelling reason to leave Dr. Black's employment and join mine?"

Bo refrained from snarling that he wasn't his secretary and sure as hell wouldn't start acting like one, but his patience was sorely tried. This little mess was already flaring his ulcer. Stomach acid had begun to churn the minute Grayson had said Penny would need some "aftercare," which was code for hospital time in the infirmary. When he saw the girl naked, spread-eagle and unconscious, his stomach went into high gear. He'd be lucky by night's end if he could choke down enough antacid to get some sleep.

"Listen, do yourself a favor…no more of these little

parties. There's a lot of heat coming down and a lot of attention on you. If you don't want to spend the rest of your life sitting in a ten-by-ten cell, you'd better start towing the line."

Grayson's stare narrowed, plainly not happy with the way Bo was talking to him, but that was too damn bad. Bo's gut ached and his head hurt and it was all because Grayson couldn't keep his extracurricular activities from doing bodily damage.

Lord help them if the FBI found Grayson's DNA on Johanna Tate's body. Damn that snot-nosed kid officer poking his nose where it didn't belong. Just one more thing to make his life difficult.

Chapter 12

Rafe received the call he'd been waiting for at 4:45 p.m., right after his last patient said goodbye.

"Someone made a good impression," Virgil said on the other line. "Ready to sign your life away in service?" he joked, but Rafe knew the jest held some truth and he was prepared. "We can't wait to put you to good work. The Saturday clinic is just the place for you, and it won't interfere with your weekday patients. Best of both worlds."

"I'm overjoyed to join the team," Rafe said, truly meaning it. One of the biggest hurdles of gaining access to records was being trusted enough to work there. He'd just been given the golden ticket. "This Saturday to start?"

"Absolutely. Come an hour or so early so I can introduce you to your team and I'll make them spring for donuts. Just don't tell Heidi. She'll have a fit about all that sugar, but once in a while isn't going to kill you, right?"

"Everything in Moderation is my motto," he said good-naturedly. "See you on Saturday, bright and early."

Rafe exited his office, still crowing about his stealth victory, and was surprised to see Darcy hadn't left. "Everything okay?" he asked, concerned.

"Actually I have a dilemma, and it's a little embarrassing."

"Oh?"

"I'm about to be homeless."

Rafe stared, not quite sure he heard her correctly. "What happened to the hotel?"

"Well, that's the thing. I used up the money I had saved for a place, and now I'll need to save up again. In the meantime, nothing has come up for rent that I could afford." He didn't like where this was going, he could see it a mile away. He was already shaking his head, but she wouldn't back down. "It would just be temporary, I promise. I'm between a rock and a hard place. I wouldn't ask if I didn't truly need a place to stay."

"I'd love to help but—"

"Would you really turn me out on the streets?" she asked, wounded.

He balked. "No, of course not, but—"

"But nothing, Rafe. I'm about to be tossed on my ear with nothing but what I came to town with, which isn't much, by the way, and you're looking like you would rather have a nail pounded into your foot than to give me temporary shelter. Come on, I won't take up a lot of room, if that's what you're worried about."

"There's no one with a room to rent?"

"Not that I've been able to find," she answered, biting her lip. His libido kicked to life and he shut it down with a ruthless shove. He didn't mind helping her out, but he was having a hard enough time fighting his attraction now, after sharing the intimate space of his cottage. She appeared piqued as she said, "You know, I'm having a hard time buying the charitable volunteer bit when you can't even let your receptionist crash on your couch for a few weeks."

Good point. His refusal did smack of hypocrisy, which he hated. He withheld a sigh and said, "You're right. Of course you're welcome to stay with me. But this is only temporary, right?"

She snorted. "Of course. Rafe, you're good-looking and all, but I'm not looking to pick out china or anything. I just need a place out of the elements."

"I have a spare bedroom," he admitted, letting loose the breath he'd been holding from apprehension. "You don't need to sleep on the couch. It's a cute place, came furnished, so I can't take the credit or the blame for the decorating."

"Great." She smiled in relief. "You're a lifesaver. I was really starting to stress. I thought you just might leave me to fend for myself, and that would've seriously damaged your good-guy image."

His mouth twisted wryly, knowing he was making— quite possibly—a terrible error in judgment and said, "I'll keep that in mind. I'll have a key made and get it to you tonight."

"Thanks," she added with a cheeky grin, "roomie."

Oh yeah…this had *bad idea* written all over it.

Darcy probably should've felt a smidge of guilt for playing Rafe so easily but this took care of two needs at once. First, she truly needed a place to live, the hotel scene was getting old and expensive; second, her gut was telling her to ferret out whatever secrets Rafe was hiding. Perhaps knowing what was driving him could lend a clue to her own puzzle. Of course this also helped with another problem she hadn't thought would be front and center right away.

That creepy police chief was stalking her…or at least it felt that way. Every time she turned around, he was heading her way. It was taking some serious evasive maneuvers to circumvent his visits, and eventually her excuses would be exhausted and she'd have to, somehow, survive the presentation to Samuel Grayson.

But seriously, yuck. Aside from the fact that she was related by blood to Samuel Grayson, she didn't find him attractive. He had a snake-oil salesman quality to him that made her skin crawl. There was something wrong about a man who made such a fuss about smiling and shaking hands when his eyes were colder than death.

What had her mother seen in the man? A pang of sadness followed. She had no idea why her mother had fallen in love with Samuel Grayson, because she hadn't been given the opportunity to know her. Were they alike in personality? Darcy was left-handed; had she inherited that characteristic from her biological mother? There were so many questions and not enough answers—not enough by a landslide.

Sometimes, like now, when she was lost in a painful melancholy over not knowing her biological mother, she felt she was betraying Louise for wanting more. In her heart, she knew that feeling was simply grief riding shotgun, disguised as guilt, but it didn't make it any easier to handle. Louise had been a wonderful mother, and Darcy had enjoyed an unencumbered childhood. That was all her biological mother had wanted, right? Well, Louise had given that to her. So why did she have this heavy knot in her chest?

A selfish part of her wished she hadn't started this journey, that she'd closed her eyes to the crazy, screwed-up world of possibilities that involved her biological parents and had just lived her life as a normal human being ignorant to the dirty truths she was bound to uncover.

But each time she imagined shouldering her pack and walking away from Cold Plains and everything it entailed, a nagging sense of unfinished business urged her to stay.

Darcy touched the pendant under her blouse, the familiar weight and feel of the St. Anthony golden medallion an instant comfort to her, not because she was overtly religious, but because Louise had given it to her during happier times on her seventeenth birthday. Just remembering that day brought a rush of bittersweet memories.

Louise had given the small, simply wrapped box to her before school. Darcy had opened it up with excitement, and when she'd lifted the medallion from the tissue, she'd smiled quizzically as her mother had never been one to cling to the dogma of organized religion. "You want me to start going to church?" she'd asked, half joking.

Louise had laughed and took it from the box to hold it up in the light. "No, silly. This is St. Anthony, the patron saint of lost things." She gestured for Darcy to turn around and lift her hair for her while she adjusted the clasp. "I figured, as often as you get lost because you have absolutely no sense of direction, you could use all the help you could get."

"M-om," she'd exclaimed, laughing. "That's not very nice."

"But true." Louise readjusted Darcy's hair so it flowed nicely over her shoulders and studied the new pendant.

There'd been a subtle wistfulness to her mother's expression that hadn't quite made sense at the time, but Darcy had naively chalked it up to Louise's reluctance to watch her baby grow up. Little had she known what a terrible secret her mother had been carrying. And now the medallion made sad sense. Darcy was the ultimate in lost things. Tears pricked her eyes and she wiped them away. Patting the medallion as if gaining strength from its molded metal, she drew a halting breath and refocused. It was time to pack. Rafe would be here soon with a key and she wanted to be ready.

Rafe helped Darcy grab her suitcase and walked toward the front door. He called over his shoulder, "It's not the Taj Mahal, but it's comfortable enough. There's a nice breeze from the trees and it's quiet." That's what he liked most, the silence. It gave him a chance to puzzle out the many pieces that fell his way without having to filter out the noise that usually surrounded him. He rounded the corner to the guest bedroom. "This is your room," he announced unnecessarily as she filed in behind him. The room was small, but at least there was enough space for a corner chair by the window, an antique nightstand and a matching dresser. It looked like an old-fashioned boarding room, like something you'd see from the 1930s. Hell, he didn't know, maybe it had been in a previous life. He hadn't cared to ask many questions when he'd been shown the rental before taking it with little fanfare. To him, it'd fulfilled basic requirements. Now, oddly, he wished he could fill the space between them with meaningless babble about the house. She gingerly bounced on the bed to test the springs. He arched his brow at the action. "Is it to your liking?"

"Perfect," she said with a smile. "To be honest, the hotel bed was a bit soft. I need support."

A dark thrill tickled at her admission and he gritted his teeth against the inappropriate imagery that happily danced in his head. Images such as how delightful it would be to throw his new "roomie" down on his king-size bed and strip her clothes from her body with his teeth. Afraid she might somehow discern the bent of his thoughts, he made for a hasty retreat but not before covering a gruff set of rules. "Any long-distance calls, I'd prefer you make on your cell phone. Feel free to make use of the kitchen and laundry room. However, please remember to clean up after yourself. I'm not a maid, nor do I have one. You do your part, I'll do mine and we'll get along just great."

"Toilet seat up or down?" she asked.

He did a double take. "What do you mean?"

"Well, you're a bachelor. I suspect you prefer the toilet seat up because there are no women in the house to consider. It's your house, so I'm being respectful. Would you like me to return the toilet seat to its upright position when I'm finished doing my business?"

She said it with such perfect seriousness, he almost didn't catch the subtle light of amusement in her eyes. In spite of himself, he actually chuckled. "Smart-ass. In deference to the lady in the house, I'll lower the seat when I'm finished. My mother would tan my hide if it were any other way, bachelor or not."

"Such a gentleman. I think I'm going to like having you as a roommate. So tell me, what's the plan for dinner? I'm starved."

"I usually grab a protein bar and some fresh fruit. I don't like to eat late. Bad for the digestion," he said, which was true but not the reason he often chewed on easy, grab-

and-go bars. He didn't want to waste the time it would take to cook something when it was just him, and each second that ticked by without finding his son was another second closer to losing him forever. However, at her look of disappointment, he said, "But I think there's enough food to scrounge up something decent, at least for tonight. Do you cook?"

"Not really," she admitted. "My mom always did the cooking. My mom's love language was food. When I was sick, she'd make fresh chicken noodle. To even suggest something from a can was an insult. She would've made my school lunches for me until I graduated if I hadn't put my foot down."

Rafe heard a hint of sadness in the deprecating laugh, but he didn't press even though he was curious. It was best to keep the lines drawn to avoid emotional entanglements. To know too much was an invitation to want more.

Like tangled sheets and rumpled clothing. His skin flushed and he wondered if the constant pressure was finally causing him to crack.

Of course he'd never expected the tension to manifest in a sexual craving that only intensified the harder he tried to smother it.

Honestly, this was ridiculous. He was a man of science, of medicine. He understood biology and the role it played in sexual attraction. Still, knowing all the ins and outs didn't nullify the tight, burgeoning ache in his groin that heralded an erection if the wind so much as blew across his trousers. "Uh...you know what? I'm sorry," he apologized, "but you're going to be on your own tonight for dinner. I just remembered I have a mountain of patient files to go over before tomorrow and I just can't spare the time. Do you mind foraging on your own?"

She smiled, puzzled by his abrupt change. "No problem. I'm good at foraging. Go ahead. You've done enough to help. Really."

Guilt for leaving her to fend for herself in his kitchen caused all manner of conflict but he knew he needed to put some distance between them. The woman tripped his switch and tempted him to do things that were out of character. Abby had been the last person to cause him to override his judgment and throw caution to the wind. If he had any fuzziness in the brain, all he had to do was pull Devin's picture from his wallet to remember everything had consequences. Not that he regretted Devin— how could he? But he'd sprinted from his old life and ran headlong into this new one, where everything felt tipped upside down and backward. He'd be lying if there weren't moments when he just wished he could close his eyes and return to his uncomplicated former existence.

"Good night," he called out, pausing by his desk to grab a stack of patient notes before disappearing into his room for the night.

He'd always considered himself a strong man, but being around Darcy reminded him that every man had a weakness.

And Darcy was fast becoming his.

Chapter 13

Darcy wandered the small, cozy house but felt wholly weird drifting around Rafe's place while he remained cloistered inside his bedroom. She wondered why he'd been so eager to get away. She tried not to let her feelings get in the way, but though she tried, she couldn't ignore the bruising of her ego. The last time she'd checked she wasn't a horrid person and certainly wasn't hard on the eyes, but Rafe maintained a defensible space between them at all times. Even when she suspected there was more to the man than he let on, that there was quite possibly a very passionate individual hidden beneath that lab coat, he did a very thorough job of stuffing that side of himself far from prying eyes. Including hers.

She realized on her third pass through the living room that there was something odd.

Nothing personal.

Not one shred of anything that would suggest that Rafe

Black lived here. The house had come furnished, but certainly Rafe had pictures of his family or other mementos with personal significance. She frowned and casually opened a few drawers in the antique buffet against the living room wall. Aside from a few dust shavings, empty. Hmm… She eyed the closed door with open speculation. The mystery of Rafe Black deepened. She'd never been much for subterfuge, which was why this venture went against the grain of her nature, but she knew she didn't have the luxury of flat-out asking him what he was hiding, so she would have to manipulate Rafe into giving her answers. But how far was she willing to go for those answers?

The answer was easy enough—she'd go as far as she had to. There was more at stake than one person's feelings. Besides, Rafe was a big boy; he could handle whatever she dished out and likely hand it right back to her with an extra serving of hot sauce on the side. A delicate ripple of awareness shuddered through her and she drew a halting breath. No doubt, she played a dangerous game.

Tapping her finger against her folded arm, she pondered her next move. She couldn't very well get answers from the man when he refused to spend more than a few minutes in her company. She had to break down those barriers and fast. The luxury of time wasn't hers, and therefore she couldn't wait for him to come around on his own.

She wasn't much of a cook, but she could whip up a nice batch of hot tea. At least that would give her an excuse to approach him instead of just standing outside his door, whining to be let in because she was lonely and out of her element.

Mug in hand, she softly knocked and held her breath. Would he ignore her? Should she knock more loudly?

How far should she take it? Don't be rude and obnoxious, she chided herself before she banged harder on the door. Maybe he was asleep....

Just as she turned to take the steaming mug back to the kitchen, the door opened and Rafe, bare chested and wearing a loose pair of soft linen shorts, stood there looking sexier than she'd ever imagined he could be. Her mouth went dry and she momentarily forgot she was holding a mug for a purpose. She thrust the cup at him, sloshing a bit like a dolt, and exclaimed as he sucked in a short breath when a hot drop landed on his midsection. "Oh God, I'm sorry," she said, distressed at her utter lack of finesse when she needed it. "I just thought you might like some tea.... I didn't mean to bother you. Here, let me get a towel."

"It's fine," he assured her, grabbing an old T-shirt draped over the hamper by the door. He rubbed the wet spot away and offered a subtle grin. "See? Easily fixed. You found everything all right?"

"Yes. The labels on the cabinets are helpful," she said, omitting the part where she'd stared incredulously at the orderly nature of his cabinets and how everything had corresponded to the label on the outside. "Are you always that organized?"

"It's a little OCD, isn't it?"

"A little." *A lot.* "However, if you're ever of a mind to start dating, you might want to disclose your penchant for labeling." She handed him the mug, this time more gently, which he accepted with a wry, almost chagrined smile that she immediately found cause for question. "What?"

"I don't drink tea."

She frowned. "Then why do you have it in your cabinet?"

"My mom always said it's good to have tea in the house for the guests who don't drink coffee."

"And do you entertain a lot of guests?"

"No." He shrugged. "Force of habit, I guess."

"Oh. Well, I'll take that back to the kitchen, then," she said, taking the mug. "Do you drink hot chocolate?"

He leaned against the doorjamb, amused. "Not typically when it's this hot. I prefer water, actually."

"Right, because of the whole soda ban," she grumbled. The first thing she'd noticed when she moved here was the absence of soda, or not that it couldn't be found, but you really had to look around. Then she found out that the drinking of soda was actively discouraged. In fact, Heidi, the nutrition Nazi, was said to go ballistic if she found out one of her patients had been sneaking the stuff on the side. "Well, I like an ice-cold soda now and then," she said, almost daring him to say something to the contrary.

With that, Rafe pushed off from the jamb and gestured for her to follow.

Intrigued, she followed him to the pantry, where he bent to retrieve something pushed to the back. He pulled out a can of cola. Her mouth watered just seeing the can, but as soon as he poured it over a glass of ice, she nearly wept with joy.

"It's like crack," she said, closing her eyes and savoring the tingling rush as the sugar and carbonation kicked her tastebuds alive. "After weeks of water and ice tea, this is heaven."

He chuckled and she opened her eyes to regard him with renewed curiosity. "A closet rule breaker, huh? Who'd have thought the buttoned-down doctor had a wild side?" Rafe didn't deny it; in fact, he seemed flattered. Emboldened, she ventured into deeper territory. "So, tell me... what about Cold Plains calls to you?"

"What do you mean?" he asked, the walls going up instantly. "I already told you. I was looking for something more meaningful to do with my life. Cold Plains seemed like it had a solid foundation in the values I believe in. Why do you find that unusual?"

"I don't," she insisted, shaking her head, but maybe she was a bit too quick with her denial, because he continued to regard her with that probing stare that made her feel stripped bare. She tucked her bottom lip against her teeth, wondering how to salvage the conversation without appearing needy, nosy or just plain obnoxious. She took a deep breath and said, "When my mom died I was searching for something to believe in, something to heal the hole in my heart. When I discovered Cold Plains, I thought I'd found that something. Then I met you. And from that moment, I've always sensed that you were searching for something, too. So, naturally, I have to wonder what you were searching for and if you found it." His mouth firmed, as if seaming shut against the urge to share what he might regret later, and she knew her window of opportunity was small. She pressed on, saying, "Rafe...I respect you're a private person and I hope I'm not pushing where I ought to butt out. However, I know how it feels to be alone in this world, and I guess what I'm trying to say is...if you need someone to talk to...I'm here."

A heartbeat passed between them and Darcy held her breath. Had she pushed too hard? His entire body seemed to vibrate with tension or maybe it was something else, but whatever it was, it was powerful enough to curl her toes and instinctively tighten the muscles in her stomach. When he started stalking toward her, slow and deliberate, as if daring her to stop him, she was too stunned to do more than just stare in anticipation.

There was no mistaking the look in his eyes—almost

feral and definitely primal—and suddenly she felt out of her league. No longer was she the one manipulating the man, and her knees turned to jelly. She managed a breathy "Rafe…" her intent to remind him that they wanted to keep lines drawn and all that nonsense, but in truth, she wanted the taste of Rafe on her tongue, the feel of his mouth possessing hers, and there was no amount of posturing and polite distancing that would stop either of them.

Alarms and bells went off in his head, but they faded with each step closer to Darcy. Was this an epically bad idea? Yes. Could he stop himself? No.

He framed her face with his hands, cupping each side tenderly, and covered her mouth with his, coaxing and demanding all at once. A dark thrill arced through him, electrifying every nerve ending, igniting a fire that devoured what was left of his common sense, incinerating any vestige of restraint he might've possessed.

Her lips, soft and giving against his, opened and their tongues tangled. He backed her against the kitchen counter until she met resistance, and she hopped onto the counter and wrapped her legs around his torso. She clutched at him, pressing her breasts against his bare chest, rubbing her hot core against his middle. He could feel the heat radiating from her center and could smell the subtle, intoxicating musk of her arousal. He wanted this woman so much his teeth ached. He cupped her butt and slid her to him. He carried her away from the counter, his mouth never leaving hers, and he took her to his bedroom.

"Wait…" she said against his mouth even as her hands curled into the short hairs of his nape. "This isn't part of our roommate agreement, is it?" she asked, pulling away to regard him with swollen lips and half-mast lids. "Because that's not what I had in mind when—"

"I know," he acknowledged with a groan, setting her down on his bed gently, the brief moment of clarity clearing the hormone-induced haze on his brain. He raked his hand through his hair, gritting his teeth against the chorus of self-recriminations reverberating in his head for losing his control when it came to Darcy. "I don't know what came over me…. I can only say it won't happen again." He went to help her up, but as she clasped his hand, she jerked him to her so he nearly fell on top of her. He startled, staring down into her eyes, confused. "What are you doing?"

"I didn't say I had a problem with it. I just want to be sure that there wasn't an expectation. If I choose to sleep with you, that's my choice. And I choose yes," she said before sealing her mouth to his, cutting off any protest to the contrary. Her tongue demanded his and he gladly gave it to her, while his hands roamed her body, learning its individual curves and valleys. Their breathing became shallow under the force of their arousal. She drew away, her stare hungry and wild. "What are you waiting for? Pants off, please."

"You first," he growled, circling her. She grinned and within seconds she'd ripped her clothes from her body to throw on the floor. At first he could only stare. Full, ripe breasts, enough for a mouthful and then some, were tipped by pebbled, mocha nipples that begged to be sucked and played with nimble fingers. His erection strained painfully, reminding him how long it'd been since he'd known the touch of a woman, and he didn't waste another moment mired in indecision. They were consenting adults. They could handle a mature conversation later about the ramifications of their actions.

He stripped and when her eyes alighted on his erection, plainly delighted with what he had to offer, he swore he might've grown a bit more.

"I knew there was something wild hiding behind that buttoned-down-doctor persona," she said, beckoning him with her finger to join her. "What else are you hiding, Dr. Black?"

He covered her with a growl. "Let me show you, Ms. Craven. I don't think you'll be disappointed."

Her skin slid beneath his fingertips as his mouth nibbled along her collarbone, dipping down to the valley of her breasts. He cupped both, slipping his tongue over the tight budded tips, burying his face between the full mounds of creamy flesh while his erection jerked, eager to sink into the hot, wet folds he fantasized about in his darkest nights. He couldn't help the moan that popped from his lips when Darcy gripped him solidly in her hand, squeezing with just the right amount of pressure to rocket his arousal onto the next plane. He rolled to his back and she popped on top, the moist heat of her center teasing the head of his erection so that he surged against her.

She laughed and wagged her finger at him. "Not so fast. I may be young but I'm not dumb. I thought you were a gentleman," she teased, her eyes twinkling in a maddeningly sexy manner that only made it more difficult for him to focus. "Me first," she instructed with a low purr that made him nearly swallow his Adam's apple. A woman who took control and knew what she wanted and wasn't afraid to ask for it... Rafe was only too happy to oblige.

They rolled again, this time with Rafe landing on top. He held both her hands above her head as he took his fill, gazing at her jutting breasts and trembling belly. How had he thought he could stay away from such a temptress, particularly now that she lived under his roof? He'd lost that fight the minute he'd agreed to this crazy idea, but at the moment, he didn't care. He offered a wolfish grin, murmuring with total pleasure, "I wouldn't have it any other way," before traveling down the length of her body to end at the juncture of her thighs. He settled at her womanly folds, nearly losing it when he heard her sharp gasp followed by a breathy moan, and then set about the task of ensuring that the lady came, not only first but again and again....

Chapter 14

Darcy awoke in Rafe's bed to the dawn cresting the horizon. She'd slept hard. Maybe she hadn't really been sleeping well at the hotel, or maybe she hadn't been sleeping well because of the recent death of her mother, but last night, she'd crashed like a drunk in lockdown.

She turned and saw, with a puzzled frown, she was alone. "Rafe?" she called out, listening for sounds of movement in the house but it was deadly silent. She checked the bedside alarm clock. It was only 5:00 a.m. He wouldn't have gone to the office so early. Would he? She gathered the comforter to her, realizing she didn't know his habits at all. Maybe he did go to the office at the crack of dawn. But to leave her like that? Without so much as a "thanks, babe" before skipping out the door? A frown gathered as her temper started to flare. *Okay, wait,* a voice that sounded a lot like her mother cautioned. She was jumping to conclusions. Darcy kicked the covers free and slid from the bed and into slippers and a robe she found on the side. Although she was tall, the robe dwarfed her in a deliciously masculine way, and the fact that it smelled like Rafe only made her want to wear it all day. *Don't go getting attached,* she told herself. *Just because you had the most amazing, knock-your-socks-off, going-to-Jesus sex of your life doesn't mean you're ready to start picking out china patterns.* She wandered into the kitchen and saw a note taped to the refrigerator door. Plucking it free, she read.

It was from Rafe. "Orange juice is in the fridge. Went for a run. Back in an hour."

"Oh goody," she said with a sigh and crumpled the paper. "A runner." Hopefully, he didn't have high hopes of her taking up the hobby now, just because they'd slept together. Darcy hated running. She did enough of it in high school in track. The track coach had taken one look at her long, gangly legs freshman year, and somehow he'd talked her into joining the team. Four years later, she'd had a handful of medals that meant nothing and a healthy aversion to lacing up her running shoes ever again. She helped herself to the orange juice and found some cream cheese to lather her bagel, and as she munched on the least healthy breakfast she'd eaten since arriving, she realized it might be a good opportunity to snoop around.

She already knew the drawers in the buffet were empty. There weren't any personal photos anywhere to hide anything behind the frames, so that left the desk. Popping the last of her bagel into her mouth, she took a seat at the flat, ugly desk that had definitely seen better days.

Darcy sifted through a few papers, found them to be ordinary household stuff and then quickly opened the drawers to see what she could find there. Neat and orderly, just like his kitchen cabinets, there were pens, paper clips and other assorted office supplies but nothing that would lift an eyebrow. She let out an annoyed sigh and realized Rafe was most definitely hiding something. No one was this organized *and* boring in their household affairs. That, in and of itself, was a red flag. His laptop sat on the desk, but she didn't dare attempt cracking it open when he could walk through the door any minute. However, something told her his laptop was likely sanitized, like his home. As she leaned back in the chair, a sudden thought came to her.

His phone. He never went anywhere without it. In fact, he was almost obsessive about knowing where his phone was at all times.

She was willing to bet her eyeteeth whatever Rafe was hiding was in that phone.

So, how was she going to get it from him without his noticing?

That was a problem for another time, she noted as Rafe walked in, his face damp from sweat and the form-fitting T-shirt clinging to his hard body. Mission discarded for the moment, she eyed him boldly. "Have a good run?"

"Not bad. I was a little tired," he admitted, sharing a private smile with Darcy as he downed the rest of his water from his water bottle and then tossed it into the recycle bin. "You sleep okay?"

"Like a baby."

"I thought so."

"Why? Are you going to tell me I snore?"

He shook his head. "No, but you do talk in your sleep."

The playful smile on her lips faded, afraid of what she might've mumbled without realizing it. "Oh? And what did I say? I'd like to point out that whatever I said doesn't mean anything and can't be held against me," she added with what she hoped was a humorous tone so as not to give away the sudden lurch in her stomach. She needn't have worried.

His chuckle lessened the tension as he said, "Nothing but incoherent mumblings. Your secrets are safe."

She smiled. *At least for the time being.* Now to tackle the elephant in the room. "So, you know things have changed, right? We can't pretend we didn't do what we did, but that's not to say that I'm looking for a relationship, so please, don't feel obligated to suddenly start opening doors for me and planning a date night. I'm fine with being a roommate with benefits, with only you and I knowing of our...special relationship."

He crossed his arms, giving a subtle frown. "That would be okay with you?"

"Of course it would. I wouldn't have brought it up if it weren't."

"That's very progressive of you," he remarked mildly, though she wasn't quite sure if he actually agreed. "And what if that arrangement doesn't work for me?"

She blinked in surprise. "Why wouldn't it? I seem to recall neither of us is looking to get involved emotionally. You're a workaholic and I'm just getting to know the community. We both have lives that are separate and we'd like to keep it that way, but that's not to say we can't enjoy each other's company now and then when the mood strikes."

It sounded good in theory. Already she could read the fatal flaws in the design, but she wasn't about to admit that to Rafe. She was sitting in his robe and wearing his slippers. She could smell him on her skin—and she liked it. She'd never believed in love at first sight, and she still didn't, but she couldn't deny the magnetic pull between them. Even now, as he stood damp with sweat and still smelling of sex from the night before, she wanted him.

Rafe caught the delicate shudder that rippled through her and his demeanor changed, narrowing with instant awareness. Her breath hitched and an unspoken exchange passed between them.

"Shower?" he murmured, his gaze never leaving hers.

She nodded slowly. He took her hand and gently pulled her from the chair, then guided her at the small of her back toward the bathroom. It was an incredibly sexy gesture that caused her heart to race and her insides to melt.

There were two sides of her, each struggling for dominance. One side was myopically focused on finding answers at any cost and the other side was more interested in spending hours in bed with Rafe, shutting out the world and everything in it.

She gasped as Rafe's mouth worked magic on her body. There was no mistaking which side was winning at the moment....

It was midafternoon when Rafe received an unpleasant surprise after enjoying a rather wonderful morning. True to her word, Darcy effectively shelved their relationship the minute they exited the front door of the house, which at first he found jarring, but then he felt this was best for both of them. Neither could afford to let anyone know that their relationship had turned personal.

Police Chief Bo Fargo walked into the office and made straight for Darcy with some semblance of a pleasant grin on his face that only made him look like a psychopath with an agenda. Rafe made an attempt to appear nonchalant at the man's appearance, but he had an idea what the visit was about, and Rafe couldn't help the surge of possessiveness that followed. "What brings you in, Chief Fargo?" he asked conversationally.

"Came to talk with the little lady here," he said, gesturing to Darcy. "Got a minute?"

Darcy shot Rafe a look, almost pleading for intervention, but he couldn't do anything overt without arousing suspicion, so he ignored the look and said, "No problem. We have a few minutes between patients."

"But I think I should stay by the phone just in case," Darcy interjected quickly with a brief, guileless smile. "Don't you agree, Dr. Black?"

Smooth girl. "Yes, that would be great. If you wouldn't mind, Chief…"

Fargo looked as if he'd just sucked a lemon but jerked a short nod anyway. "Yeah, I'll make it quick," he groused, returning to Darcy. Rafe made a show of perusing a patient file, but in truth, he was keenly listening to the exchange.

"You're a hard girl to find," Fargo said, his voice low and vaguely accusatory. "Two weeks ago, I talked to you about meeting with Mr. Grayson. He's a very important man and he's eager to make your acquaintance. Aren't you excited about meeting our town's most important resident?"

Rafe grit his teeth, wanting to put his fist through Fargo's fleshy mouth for being Grayson's lapdog and servant boy.

"Most important? I thought the mayor got top billing in most towns," she teased.

"Well, Cold Plains is special," Fargo said. "We do things differently."

"Yes, I've noticed."

"So, when can I tell Mr. Grayson you'll see him?"

"Well…"

"He's real eager, and he's a busy man," Fargo said, pressing her.

It took everything in Rafe not to interject. In fact, he was nearly biting his tongue in half. But he needn't have worried. Darcy was tougher than she looked.

"I'll let you know. I'm really busy here with work and I'm still just feeling my way around town. I'm sure I'm bound to bump into him eventually. It's a pretty small town."

Rafe chanced to look up and caught Fargo's jowly face flush and his stare narrow in thinly disguised anger, but Darcy seemed not to notice she was treading on dangerous ground. Maybe that was her saving grace because Fargo dialed it down and said with a shrug, "Suit yourself. Just don't wait too long. Mr. Grayson meets a lot of people. You don't want to miss out on making an impression."

"Duly noted, Chief," she said sweetly.

Fargo tipped his hat in a desultory manner and left the building. Rafe let the tension flow from his shoulders and released the breath he hadn't realized he'd been holding. He caught Darcy's gaze and she smirked.

"You handled yourself well," he said.

"No thanks to you. What gives? That guy is a creep. He's been stalking me for days. And what's the deal with this Grayson guy? He meets everyone new in town?"

"He meets every woman in town," Rafe clarified, frowning at her preceding statement. "If I'd come rushing to your rescue, Chief Fargo would've been suspicious, and I don't need anyone questioning my loyalty to Cold Plains."

"And why is that, exactly?"

He leveled his stare at her. "It's personal."

"Isn't everything?" she countered, not deterred. But

that was as far as she got because a patient walked in. Her mouth firmed as if disappointed at being interrupted, but she turned away from Rafe, and he heard the welcoming smile in her voice as she greeted his patient.

He smothered a smile, inappropriate to the situation, but Darcy was something else. He'd never met a woman who could switch on and off like she could. Maybe she ought to work for the CIA, he mused before heading to the exam room to meet with his patient. Funny thing about that quality, though. If she could shut off whatever she was feeling at that moment, how was he to know what was fake and what was real?

Chapter 15

For the time being, Darcy felt she'd put Chief Fargo off for a bit, but she didn't doubt that he'd come around again eventually. Darcy was starting to get a feel for what went on around this town and she was universally squicked out over the idea of being paraded in front of some guy in the hopes of impressing him enough for him to bed her. But she'd done a little research into cults before landing in Cold Plains and had even studied such men as Jim Jones, David Koresh and assorted other nut jobs who fancied themselves leaders of their communities. Her daddy-o certainly fit the bill from what she could tell: egotistical, narcissistic and suffering from a God complex. Well, she didn't know about the God complex, but she wouldn't be surprised. The very fact that Chief Fargo was intent on presenting her to Grayson like a subject in the king's realm was proof enough for her that Grayson was running a ship of fools and he was the captain.

So what was so personal to Rafe that he couldn't stick up for her when she needed it? She'd known that he wanted to, she'd seen it in the tension cording his shoulders, yet he'd remained silent. Would he have let Fargo drag her out of there, kicking and screaming? She scowled. It certainly didn't jibe with that gentlemanly vibe she'd gotten earlier. Of course, they had mucked things up by sleeping together. It complicated things, even though they both talked a good game about keeping their relationship professional during the day, no matter what they did at night.

What a bunch of horse dookie. Darcy sent a prayer skyward to her mother, hoping Louise noticed how she refrained from using her word of choice in that instance, but it certainly didn't feel as satisfying.

She busied herself with straightening her desk, but questions remained no matter how hard she pushed them aside. It really bothered her that Rafe had done nothing to deter Fargo. She didn't expect him to be her knight in shining armor, but for crying out loud, she didn't think he'd be the kind of man to look the other way when a woman was in trouble.

Darcy drummed her fingers lightly against the surface of the desk, her thoughts in a tangle. *Oh, who cares why Rafe didn't rise to the occasion,* she argued with herself. She was here to find answers about her mother, not moon after some guy because he didn't rise to her level of expectation in the chivalry department.

It was all well and good to use logic to talk herself down from an emotional snit, except anyone who has tried knows when you're in an emotional state, logic means nothing.

So when the day came to an end, and she and Rafe went

home, her bruised feelings had morphed into real anger, and she'd be the first to admit logic had lost the fight hours ago.

"Hey, I thought since I bailed on dinner last night, maybe I could redeem myself and fix something tonight. I make a mean quesadilla."

Darcy shot him a cold look. "I'm not hungry."

"Oh. Okay. Well, a rain check, then, I suppose?"

She exhaled a short irritated breath. Was he actually trying to make small talk as if he hadn't totally *failed* earlier today? Either he had an incredibly short memory or he was hoping she did. "Let's cut the crap, Rafe. I'm not in the mood."

Rafe wisely refrained from countering with something snide, which she gave him points for, but she wasn't in the mood to give him much more. But then he went and ruined things by calling her out.

"What's your problem?" he asked as they entered the house.

Good, she thought. *No beating around the bush. Let's get to the point.*

"I'm pissed at you," she stated flatly.

He did a double take. "Why?"

"Why?" *Oh, how quickly men forget when they've been an ass.* The cynic in her was alive and well and in charge, it seemed. "Because you threw me to that wolf in sheep's clothing, Fargo. Forget the fact that we've knocked boots, put that aside for just a minute, and let's go with plain human decency. How could you let that pig of a man try to bully me into going with him to meet Samuel Grayson? You know the only reason he wants to meet me is to sleep with me. Is that okay with you? Because, personally, I think it's disgusting. Do you step aside every time Fargo comes sniffing around the new girls? What kind of man are you?" The last part came out in a spat of disgust, and Rafe's nostrils flared as his stare hardened as tightly as his jaw. His quick stride caught her by surprise as he gripped her arms. "Ouch!" she exclaimed but she was startled by the darkness in his eyes.

"I don't know what's going on between us—something I didn't want to happen, but it did anyway—but when Fargo came in and started talking to you about Grayson, I wanted to bury my fist in his fat mouth, but I don't have that luxury. The thought of you going anywhere near Grayson makes me want to hurt someone, but that's an irrational reaction that I can't afford." He loosened his grip abruptly as if realizing how hard he'd been grabbing her arm, but his eyes remained hot, even if Darcy could tell he regretted his actions. "You don't know what's at stake for me, so don't go making judgments without all the facts."

"And whose fault is that, that I don't know everything? Tell me, what are you hiding? I know it's something, because you're too damn perfect in a town full of nuts, and you're up to something, I can tell. The question is, are you in with them or you doing something else entirely? I need to know."

"You're full of questions for a woman who seems to have her own secrets. No one just shows up at Cold Plains without a reason. You've already stated Grayson doesn't charm you like he does everyone else. And you're not really interested in the Cold Plains lifestyle. There's something you're not saying, either."

She shrugged. "So we both have secrets."

"Yeah, I guess so."

"But that doesn't explain why you didn't stick up for me."

"You're a grown woman and it seemed you handled yourself pretty well," he said.

"Yes, because if I hadn't, I think that Fargo would've dragged me out by my hair. Would you have done something then?"

Rafe's mouth tightened with anger, but she didn't care. Her feelings were hurt, and she'd been sorely disappointed by his actions—or inaction, as it were, and she didn't care if she was being irrational.

"I told you why I didn't say anything," he said in a steely tone. "I can't afford raising suspicion. Fargo already has me on his radar. I can't take the risk of being in his crosshairs. Lives could be put in danger."

That caught her attention. "What do you mean?"

"I can't—"

"Can't or won't?"

"This conversation is going nowhere good. We should just drop it. You're angry I didn't come to your rescue. I get it. I'm sorry. It was a risk I couldn't take. Let's leave it at that."

Darcy's eyes stung at his blunt admission. Why did she care so much? She looked away before he could catch the shine, but he caught it anyway. He started to say something, but she cut him off with a jerk of her head, saying, "Forget it. Never mind. I don't care. It was stupid even to bring it up." She moved to escape to her bedroom, but Rafe stopped her, his demeanor softening. He pulled her into his arms, which she resisted but only marginally. She wanted his comfort, wanted him to apologize and mean it, not that perfunctory, angry, tossed-out sentiment.

"I'm sorry," he said softly, his voice heavy with regret. His chest felt warm and perfect against her cheek and she wondered how she could want someone the way she wanted Rafe in such a short amount of time. Back home, she'd dated men for weeks and not felt this kind of connection. It baffled her and certainly didn't make things easier for her in her mission. She buried her nose against his body and drew a long breath, trying to hold back the tears, which weren't far away. Rafe smoothed the hair on her crown to frame her face so that she stared up at him. "I...don't want anyone else touching you, Darcy. Frankly, I don't think you should stay in this town. Cold Plains can be a dangerous place, and sometimes the most treacherous element isn't the most obvious. I want you to be safe and that's not something I can guarantee here."

She wiped her nose. "There's no guarantee of safety anywhere, Rafe. I could walk out in front of a bus and die right there. If it's my time, it's my time."

"There aren't many buses in Cold Plains," he said gravely. "But there are far worse hazards, trust me."

"Why do you stay if it's so dangerous?" she asked.

He took a long moment to answer, as if weighing his decision to share. She held her breath, needing to know almost as much as he needed to keep it secret. Finally, he said in a low, pained voice, "My son is missing and I think he's here somewhere in Cold Plains. I'm trying to find him before it's too late."

Darcy's jaw fell open. Of all the things he might've said...she hadn't seen that one coming.

Rafe held his breath, not quite sure why he'd shared his personal motivation with a woman he hardly knew, but somehow it'd felt right to tell her. It wasn't exactly common knowledge in the community that he was looking for his son. He preferred to keep that information on a need-to-know basis, but telling Darcy felt like something he needed to do.

"A son?" she repeated, staring, her confusion evident. "You're a father?" At his nod, she said, "You don't have any pictures anywhere of him. Of anyone, for that matter. This is the most…impersonal living space I've ever seen. Why don't you have any pictures of him?"

Rafe stepped away, knowing he'd already spilled the beans. There was no sense in holding back now, but it was still hard for him to talk about. "I had a…one-night stand about a year ago at a medical conference. I met Abby Michaels there. We had a few drinks and one thing led to another and we spent the night together. I never saw her again but I received a phone call—a frantic one from Abby—saying she'd given birth to my son and that they were in danger. I wired her some money and then we were supposed to meet at this old diner outside of Laramie. She never showed. Then she turned up dead, but Devin—that's my son's name—wasn't with her. I've been searching for him ever since."

It was a bombshell to absorb, so when Darcy took a long moment to respond, he didn't fault her. He could only imagine what was going through her head.

"Why Cold Plains?"

Here goes another leap of faith that she isn't a Devotee, Rafe thought with a jangle to his nerves. "Abby was linked to Samuel Grayson. She may have been one of his 'girls.'"

"Oh…" The full ramification of his revelation sank in and she shuddered. "What about the cops? Do they know this? Why haven't they arrested him or, at the very least, brought him in for questioning?"

"It's complicated," he said grimly. "His alibi is clear by

cops' standards, and there's no actual proof that Samuel Grayson killed her."

Darcy looked up sharply. "You think he killed her?"

"If he didn't pull the trigger, he at least knows who did. Nothing happens in this town without Grayson knowing about it."

"How do you know Devin is your son and not Grayson's?"

In answer, Rafe pulled the photo from his wallet and handed it to Darcy. Her stare widened. "He looks just like you," she observed incredulously. "He's like your mini-me. Guess your DNA is pretty strong."

He took the photo and tucked it back into his wallet. "Now you know why I know why he's mine."

"Good-looking boy," she said, almost shyly. "I mean, for a baby, because, no offense, I think they all look kinda alike. Except yours, of course."

He smiled, but his heart remained heavy. Sometimes just looking at the photo made him want to claw his chest out. He'd never held that boy in his arms, never seen him smile or heard him coo, but he loved him. He knew that for certain, and each day that ended with a dead end only sharpened the pain Rafe lived with every day.

"I have to find my boy, and to do that, I have to play the game to get close to the people who might know who's keeping him."

Darcy's eyes watered and she wiped away the moisture with a jerky nod. "I understand. I'm sorry for being such an insensitive twit. And you're right, I can take care of myself. I just—" she drew a deep, shuddering breath "—wanted you to care, I guess."

Rafe pinned her with a steady stare that she felt to her toes and assured her in a low and desperate growl that was both sexy and honest, "I do care. Too much, Darcy. You have no idea how I wanted to keep my distance from you, because I knew I wouldn't be able to keep you at arm's length like I should."

She understood that sentiment, suffered through it herself. But she'd never been good at following advice, even when it was her own.

Rafe pulled her to him, gently twisting her arm behind her to rest their twined hands at her back. It was an incredibly sexy and dominant move that reminded her that she was a woman first and foremost and terribly attracted to this man who should be off-limits.

He kissed her deeply, sweeping her mouth with a probing touch of his tongue, bending her to him in a way that left no confusion as to what he wanted to do to her, and she eagerly accepted. Rafe's touch turned insistent and soon they were pulling each other's clothes off, impatient to feel each other's skin against the other.

Darcy feasted her gaze on Rafe's body, fairly certain she'd never tire of watching or touching the lean muscle rippling beneath his skin. Tight abs connected to a lean waist and hips, and it was all Darcy could do to stop from staring like a starving woman at an all-you-can-eat buffet.

"If you don't stop looking at me like that, this is going to be over real quick," he warned in a sexy growl, climbing her body and sucking at the tender, sensitive skin at her neck. She gasped and clutched at the muscled flesh of his ass, encouraging him without words that she liked what he was doing. She wrapped her legs around his torso, thrilling at the insistent press of his erection against the hot center of her body.

"Who said there was anything wrong with fast and furious?" she said, her playful smile going slack with desire when Rafe's mouth latched on to her nipple, drawing the tip with single-minded attention. She twisted under his ministrations, deliberately intent upon forgetting the precarious situation facing them both. All that mattered was now. Reality would intrude soon enough.

Rafe covered Darcy's body, every nerve ending going off in raucous starbursts of sensation, every inch of skin touching hers warm and alive. The need to possess her, feel her, consumed him like an uncontrollable fire from within that incinerated reason and good judgment. Her insistent hands roamed his body as his mouth traveled hers. She held in her hand the power to destroy everything he'd built, but he couldn't regret telling her about Devin. He'd been compelled to share, as if knowing the burden would be easier to bear if only she was there to bear it with him, and though he knew logically that reasoning was built on a foundation of shifting sand, he had to believe he'd made the right choice.

"Now, Rafe," she pleaded in a low, throaty voice that slid along his mind like a stroke on his erection. He jerked, his thoughts a babbling mess of *want it, need it, gotta have it,* and he gratefully slid into her slick and ready folds with a groan that rattled from his toes. She clutched at him, drawing him deeper, urging him to go *harder, faster,* and it was all he could do not to spill right then and there.

"Oh God, Darcy…" he gasped, shaking the bed with each piston thrust into her body, losing all sense of time and space. This was unlike anything he'd ever known. He felt wildly out of control, frenzied by the intense connection between them. It was more than random coupling, a satisfying of need. He could feel her heartbeat against his, the way her body cleaved to his with each shuddering breath. Had he ever known such blinding pleasure? The answer was easy enough as he came in a hurtling shot, his orgasm momentarily stopping his heart until it kick-started a second later with a wild thrash of life-affirming rhythm.

He rolled to his back, slowly returning to earth, stunned. Darcy's breath came fast and shallow, as soft moans rode the receding waves of her own orgasm. *Had they—?* Awareness came gradually, but when it did, Rafe turned to Darcy in alarm, realization in his stare, but words weren't necessary. Her expression mirrored his.

"We didn't…" she started, her cheeks still riding high with flushed color. "Oh no…"

Rafe's stare drifted to the ceiling. "No, we didn't," he returned grimly, wondering how he could be so stupid again. There was no excuse. He knew better. Damn it! He returned to her, an apology on his tongue, but how do you appropriately put into words an apology for not using a condom? He might've just gotten her pregnant. Holy hell….

He must've turned a shade of white, for Darcy caressed his face with concern, even though he could read the apprehension clearly in her own expression. "I'm sure it'll be fine," she said. "I'm not in the right time in my cycle." She tried a smile for his benefit. "Besides, I read somewhere that it's actually pretty difficult to get pregnant. There's only a small window to hit the mark. What are the odds that you hit that mark the first time we don't use a condom?"

He shot her a derisive look. "My odds have been pretty good so far."

"Well, let's not borrow trouble. Think positive." She swung her legs over the edge of the bed and popped up, heading for the bathroom, saying over her shoulder before disappearing, "For the record, that was *amazing*. Repeat performances are requested and appreciated, Dr. Black." She winked and shut the door.

Chapter 16

Rafe's first Saturday at the clinic, he played every inch the part of the helpful, eager volunteer. He smiled, even engaged in flirty banter—something he never would've done in his old life when he was hyperfocused on his career and not at all on chasing the skirts around the hospital, like some doctors were known to do. But for every false smile he offered in the hopes of charming away any suspicion, Rafe took careful note of details all around. Unlike the men who simply used the women around him, particularly nurses, Rafe had always known that the nurses were the backbone of a working hospital. They knew the ins and outs, knew which doctors weren't worth the paper their medical license was printed on and which doctors they'd choose if their own family members' lives were at stake. They knew who was sleeping with whom and who was secretly stocking their own private pharmaceutical stores. In short, nurses were like an in-hospital network of the deepest connections, and Rafe wanted to make friends within that system.

It was near the end of his first shift, and Rafe was itching to have a look around without eyes on him at all times. Although friendly, there was still a barrier, a "watch and see" attitude he had to circumvent. He needed them to let down their guard so he could roam unencumbered through this cavernous modern building. He tried to make small talk with some of the staff, even the janitor, but everyone kept to their roles pretty firmly. Of course he knew it would take time, but his impatience made him antsy. It finally came to the point where he had to leave or else draw suspicion, so he made his way to the locker room to grab his stuff. It was there he found the OB ward chief, Dr. Rolf Bulger, an older man with a balding pate and a thick Hungarian accent, who seemed an odd choice for an obstetrics ward, but Rafe realized he was sharp after only an hour in his company.

Bulger finished changing his shoes and looked up to acknowledge Rafe.

"You're good," he said with a short grunt as he stood. He added with a clap on Rafe's shoulder and a weary expression, "You are a godsend. I've been asking for help for some time now but never help does it come."

"I offered as soon as I arrived in Cold Plains," Rafe told Bulger, spreading his hands in a helpless gesture. "But I guess I had to wait for the right time."

"Bah. Approval nonsense. I'm being run ragged without the help I was promised, but nobody cares." Rafe quietly took note of the open bitterness in Bulger's tone, wondering where Bulger stood in Grayson's army. No one spoke with such outward criticism against the Cold Plains way. Was Bulger someone Rafe could trust? If so, why would

Grayson put someone on the outside in charge of the OB ward? For that question alone, Rafe knew to bide his time and hold his tongue. One careless slip, and everything could come crashing down. He couldn't afford such a mistake.

Bulger eyed him speculatively. "What's your story, Black? Are you looking for purpose or something like that?"

Rafe smiled. "Something like that."

Bulger waved away his enigmatic answer, irritation written in plain lines across his face. "Keep your secrets. I'm up to my eyeballs in intrigue. Your shift is up. You do good work. Whatever your motivation, the help is appreciated. Do you plan to return? Can I count on you?"

Rafe nodded. "Absolutely. I enjoyed volunteering in the OB ward. It seems Cold Plains is blessed with fertile families."

"Yes," Bulger grunted. "Successful, it is."

"Successful?"

Bulger stopped short, as if realizing he'd said more than he should, but recovered with a shrug. "This English is still not my strength…. I mean, healthy babies…is good, yes?"

"I'd say so," Rafe agreed, but what about the unhealthy babies? Where'd they go? He didn't see a NICU. "Where do the preemies go? Are they transported to a pediatric hospital elsewhere?"

"We have state-of-the-art facility here. No need for transporting tiny babies. They grow, thrive, here. But you don't worry about such things. I would not put you with the preemies. You work with healthy mothers and babies. That's the best place for you. Leave the rest to me."

"I'll go wherever I'm needed," Rafe said, leaving it at

that, but his mind was moving quickly. Bulger all but admitted there was a special ward for babies who were different in some way, whether premature or sickly. Where was that ward? And why was there so much secrecy? Earlier, he'd heard frightful whispers that imperfection of any kind set Grayson's teeth on edge, and Rafe had to wonder if that rumor didn't have a grain of truth. Grayson was such an odd duck, frankly, Rafe wouldn't put anything past the man. Was Devin imperfect in some way? Was that why Grayson kept him secreted away? If that were the case, Rafe didn't care what perceived imperfection Devin suffered from; the boy belonged with him and he'd do whatever it took to bring him home.

"Time to call it a night," Rafe announced, grabbing his keys and wallet from the locker. "See you next Saturday?"

"Yes. I look forward to working with you again, Dr. Black. You seem good, smart. We need more like you. Too many dumb and weak in this place."

Rafe didn't know how to safely respond, so he simply smiled and waved before leaving the locker room.

Rolf Bulger looked as sour as if he'd sucked a lemon for dinner instead of the filet mignon that'd been prepared earlier in preparation for this meeting. Samuel suppressed the urge to snap at the older man, irritated at the peevish stance he'd taken in regard to Samuel's extracurricular activities. The tension in the room had grown to the point that there were nervous shuffles and cleared throats whenever Rolf started to speak, but the old fart wouldn't be silenced, not this time.

"This is going too far, Samuel," Rolf said, his brows drawn in a thunderous line. "You are becoming a menace and foolish, to boot. You cannot keep doing this and expect no one to notice. These are babies, for Chrissakes!"

"Babies no one knows about," Samuel retorted coolly, shooting Fargo a look. The good doctor was fast becoming a pain in his side. He didn't care to be schooled, by him or anyone. This was his town, and it seemed the doctor needed to be reminded who signed his paycheck. "What seems to be the problem?" he asked, settling in his chair with his glass of champagne. They were supposed to be celebrating, and yet Rolf was bringing down the mood with his whining. "I've heard no complaints...." He looked to Fargo for confirmation, which Fargo supplied with a jerk of his head. "See? There are no complaints from the women. Most are happy to be free of the burden of pregnancy. It's a win-win, and everyone remains happy in our beautiful little oasis."

"What about the ones who wanted to keep their babies? Huh? What of them?" Rolf shot back, a speck of spittle flying in his exuberance. Samuel's lip curled in disgust. He hated spit. He started to speak but Rolf wasn't finished. "Forced abortions...it's not right! They didn't even know what had happened to them. You make me lie to these women, saying their babies had died in utero, all because they might've been yours. Oh yes, I know! I know what you do to these women and I know about these women who don't come back from the infirmary. It's sick! I won't have any part of it any longer!"

Fargo tensed, his fingers moving to his sidearm. Samuel stilled him with a murmured word, returning to Rolf, who was trembling with his outrage, his sense of conviction. The rest of the room had stilled, watching in rapt interest and perhaps fear. Samuel needed to take control before Rolf shot off like the loose cannon he'd become.

He smiled, trying to calm the older man. "Rolf, there is no one in this room I respect more," he lied easily, seeking to charm the older man. "I hear your concern and it pains me that you are so bothered by the choices that have been made for the good of the community."

"It's for your own selfish gain, not the community," Rolf countered in a low voice, seeking confirmation from the rest of the group but coming up empty. No one spoke out against Samuel so foolishly. Rolf's old blue eyes registered sharp disappointment and even disgust at everyone's reluctance, but he didn't back down, the pain in the ass. "This has to stop," he said.

"We've discussed this, Rolf," Samuel said with all the patience he didn't feel. Yet he needed to pull off this charade. "I cannot have women claiming to have my offspring. I cannot be tied to one woman, one family. I belong to Cold Springs. My focus is the community. I am every child's father."

"At this rate, you will be," Rolf groused under his breath.

Damn bastard. Samuel narrowed his stare but continued, his voice losing some of its kindness. "Enough. You have lost focus. You're overworked. Once you have some rest, you'll remember everything is done to the community's greater good. You were on board with the lifestyle at one time. You will be again. You just need to be reminded of your priorities."

"Damn your—"

"Chief," Samuel interrupted in a hard tone. "Please escort the good doctor to his car. He's finished here this evening. The doctor needs his rest."

Fargo approached the older man, who stared at the thick chief of police with a smidge of fear in his defiant stare.

That's right, you old coot. I have the power and you have none. A lesson you'd do well to remember. He smiled as Fargo forcibly helped the doctor from the room, leaving Samuel with the rest of his closest community members. He addressed the situation immediately, choosing to slay the elephant in the room before it rampaged out of control. He affected a contrite expression. "It seems there's been some question as to how I've been handling the unfortunate situation with unwanted pregnancies. As you know, unwanted pregnancies are a blight on a community, something we strive to eradicate whenever we encounter it, for the good of Cold Plains. Trust me when I say that these young ladies were more than happy to be afforded a second chance at living the life they choose instead of being tied down with an unwanted child, born out of wedlock, without benefit of both mother and father. To my knowledge, none of the ladies were ones I'd spent time with," he lied smoothly. Most were. He detested using a condom. He liked knowing there was nothing standing between his flesh and theirs, which meant, at times, the women conceived. He always slipped a morning-after pill in their drinks later, but sometimes, Mother Nature proved to be tricky. And the woman started getting soft and fat around the waist. He shut down the shudder of distaste and affected a warm smile. "Cold Plains means everything to me. All I do is for the good of the community. If you trust in nothing else, trust in that."

Relieved smiles broke out on faces throughout the room, and he knew he'd circumvented a potentially sticky issue. However, even as he smiled and shook hands as people filed out of the secret room built into the community center, he realized Fargo had been right. He couldn't afford to play so decadently for the time being. More attention from the feds or that snot-nosed officer bent on pinning Johanna's murder on him would only serve to destroy everything he'd so painstakingly built thus far.

Thoughts of Penny, his most recent assistant and bed partner, jumped to mind and he realized damage control was necessary. He made a mental note to visit the girl in the infirmary, to play the part of a man genuinely devastated over his actions. He hadn't meant to hurt her; her beauty had spurred him to a frenzy, he'd tell her. He'd carefully selected young Penny for her seemingly wild streak, knowing he could push her further than anyone else. And if she didn't buy his contrite act and threatened to tell, he'd just have to produce his ace.

He smiled. Was it brash of him to hope that she would threaten to tell Officer McCall how Samuel had practically raped her while she'd been tied helplessly to his bed? How else was he supposed to watch the color drain from her face when he showed her the pictures and video that'd been taken from a hidden location in his bedroom? How the videos showed, in full, nasty detail, how she'd been squealing and grunting with pleasure as he'd done unspeakably dirty things to her with full consent? Perhaps her parents would like a copy? Of course the segment of the video where he'd beaten her nearly to death was edited out. It would be her word against his, with damning evidence to the contrary. He'd paint her out to be a liar and a whore. And no one would be the wiser. He chuckled, his step light. It was good to be the king. Indeed, it was.

Chapter 17

Through the grace of God, Rafe managed to go through the motions of meeting with his regular patients, but his mind was traveling the corridors of the clinic, mentally strategizing his next move.

Saturday loomed and he couldn't wait. Darcy noticed his preoccupation and called him on it that Friday night after they'd suffered through a bout of Darcy's cooking, in spite of Rafe's offer to take the lead in the culinary department.

"What's going on with you?" she asked. "Surely my cooking wasn't that bad?"

It was, but his thoughts were far from the indigestion he'd likely experience later. "Work stuff," he lied, not wanting to involve Darcy more than needed. Although he'd shared his fears with her, he'd edited how deep he was going into this charade for the sake of his son. If he told her he was trying to find a way to infiltrate the clinic, she'd likely try to help, and he didn't want to risk her getting hurt. He was dealing with thugs, even if they smiled and seemed neighborly on the outside. In a short time, Darcy had managed to get under his skin and he couldn't shoulder another fear that he might lose someone he cared about. He smiled and pushed a stray hair from her eyes. "It's nothing. So, here's a question for you," he said, turning the focus away from him for a moment. "Why are you really in Cold Plains? You never really answered the question, and it seems only fair that you tell me what's going on from your angle when you know what I'm all about."

She pulled away, a small smile fixed on her lips. "That's not entirely true," she said. "Somehow I'm guessing that I don't know the whole story. You're a deep-well kind of guy, not a shallow pool."

Rafe stilled, surprised at how quickly she'd gained insight into his character. Her keen attention to detail both impressed and frightened him. He'd have to be careful around her. A part of him wished he could just pack up, Darcy included, and get the hell out of this place before they both ended up doing the dirt dance. But that wouldn't help Devin. That wouldn't solve anything. Agent Bledsoe was counting on him to help behind the scenes and he couldn't let him down, not when he was working his ass off to bring Samuel Grayson down. He was willing to stand behind anyone dedicated to that single goal. "Finding my son is my sole focus," he said, which was the truth. "Every night that goes by without finding him is like a knife in my heart. I'm scared that no matter how hard I search, it'll be too late. He could be dead already."

Her brows furrowed at the pain that leached from his voice and she caressed his jaw. "Don't say that," she murmured. "You have to keep hope alive. Think positive and don't let doubt enter into your mind—it'll drag you down. My mom used to tell me that angels listened to our prayers even when we didn't say them out loud. But you know, you have to help them out. Tell yourself that you will find Devin. That he will be in your arms soon. Those are the prayers that matter and need to be heard."

He was struck by the fierce nature of her declaration. And by her caring. He leaned in and pressed a soft, firm kiss to her lips. He drew away. How was it possible she became more beautiful with each passing day? Her mouth tipped into a sweetly playful smile and he knew he'd do anything to protect her from Samuel Grayson. She meant so much to him, to his sanity. For the first time since arriving in Cold Plains, he didn't feel failure nipping at his heels, desperate despair around every corner.

She smoothed the frown that had begun to build and said, "Hey, no more sadness. If it makes you feel better, whatever domestic urge possessed me to attempt cooking dinner has passed. Generally speaking, I only get those urges once in a while. So I think you're safe for at least a year."

"Speaking of urges," he murmured, thinking she'd never looked sexier dressed in sweats and a ratty T-shirt and that he couldn't wait to get her out of them. "Want to work off that dinner?"

She grinned and wrapped her arms around his neck. "Absolutely. I need my cardio."

Darcy listened to the slow, even breathing of Rafe beside her and fought the urge to shake him awake so she could confess the secret she was carrying. But even as she reached for him, she pulled back, knowing that nothing good would come of sharing with Rafe. He was an incredibly decent man; why should she burden him with the knowledge that he was sleeping with the daughter of the man responsible for killing the mother of his child? Would he recoil in horror that Grayson's DNA flowed through her veins? She could barely stand the knowledge herself; how was he supposed to feel about it? She rolled to her back, wondering how she'd come to be in this position. She cared about Rafe. Deeply. It wasn't supposed to happen that way. She'd thought she could manipulate Rafe into giving her some answers, maybe provide a buffer between herself and that creep, Fargo, but somewhere along the line, she'd handed Rafe her heart, without even realizing it. It felt completely natural to be in his bed, snuggled against his body, eating dinner together and essentially playing house. *Playing house?* Whose life was she living? She was no closer to finding answers about her mother, and now she'd gone and fallen in love with a man who was embroiled in his own drama. She ought to leave. Walk away from it all, Rafe included. The very thought, whispered in her mind, caused a painful spasm across her chest. *Well, there you have it,* she noted wryly. She was in love. *Fabulous.* Darcy scooted closer to Rafe and spooned against him, discontent with the knowledge that her life had changed forever and wondrously at home pressed against this man, who, incidentally, was still hiding something from her.

Oh yes, she could sense it. She supposed he was trying to protect her. That was Rafe, looking out for everyone, ever the healer. But he didn't know her well enough yet to know that she wasn't easily tucked under someone's wing, whether it was for her protection or not. Her mother had said it was one of her few faults—a stubborn determination to do things her way, no matter the consequence.

And knowing he wasn't going to let her in on whatever was troubling him, she'd just have to find out herself.

Whether he liked it or not…she would help him find his son.

Darcy had to chuckle at the irony: she was staking out Officer Ford McCall. She waited until he exited his Escalade—department issue? Seems those $25 bottles of water were paying for more than clean streets—and then when he was safely inside the coffee shop, she quietly slid in the passenger side. How many people actively sought to climb *into* a police car? Not many, which worked in her favor. She scooted down so no one saw her chilling in McCall's vehicle, and when he opened the door to climb in, he actually jumped and reached for his sidearm when he saw her hiding in his vehicle. "Wait!" she exclaimed, gesturing for him to hold up. "I have a really good explanation for why I'm in your car," she promised, earning a confused scowl on his part. "Just get in, pretend all is well and we'll chat. I didn't want your boss seeing me with you."

That seemed to make a certain amount of sense, because Ford relaxed his itchy trigger finger and turned the ignition. As he pulled out of the parking lot, his eyes never leaving the road, he said, "Okay, start talking, and just because you're cute doesn't mean you aren't crazy, so you'd better have a really good reason for carjacking me."

She snorted. "You're definitely a country boy. This is not a carjacking," she said, her comment earning a deeper scowl, telling her he wasn't amused but at least he was curious. And he hadn't driven straight to the station to lock her up. Talk about taking chances. She went with her gut feeling that Ford wasn't a Devotee. If she was wrong…

she didn't want to think about it. "Go to the Hanging Tree. We'll talk there."

Ford made a U-turn and started to head out of town. "And how do you know about the Hanging Tree? That's a local thing," he said, gunning the engine as soon as they were clear of town. "You're something else, Ms. Craven. I bet the doc's got his hands full with you."

You have no idea. "I'm sorry for *carjacking* you, but I didn't want to be seen chatting. No offense, but I seem to have caught the radar of your creepy boss and I didn't want to deal with the fallout. He's gotten it into his head that I want to knock boots with Samuel Grayson, which I definitely *do not.* The very idea makes me nauseous," she muttered, more to herself than Ford, but he got the picture.

Ford nodded, and within a few minutes, they were at the Hanging Tree. He made sure they were alone and then gestured for her to climb off the floorboard. "Okay. Spill it. What's this about?"

"Before I say anything, answer me this. Are you one of those crazy Devotees?"

He cocked his head at her. "And what if I was? Wouldn't that put you in deep right about now? Secluded place, openly disparaging the Cold Plains way?"

She swallowed and nodded. "Yeah. Right about now, I'm wishing I hadn't had that last latte. Just answer the question, please."

Ford regarded her with open scrutiny, and just when she thought she'd royally screwed up, he shook his head slowly. "No. I'm not a Devotee. And I don't aim to be one, neither. Ever. Folks aren't right in the head who blindly follow Samuel Grayson." He didn't give her a chance to exhale in relief, following with, "What's your story? Why aren't you gaga over the man like most other women?"

"I'm his daughter," she said, cringing at the sound of the words falling from her mouth. Had she just blithely told Ford McCall when she hadn't told Rafe? Yeah, there was that, but circumstances were a bit different, she rationalized to herself. She wasn't sleeping with Ford McCall, nor did she care what he thought of her. She cared about Rafe…a lot.

"Daughter?" Ford repeated, disbelief evident, and she didn't blame him. Then the realization hit him like a ton of bricks. He snapped his fingers in recognition. "That's why you looked familiar. Damn, I don't know why I didn't see it before. You're his spitting image."

"Yes, lucky me, but you can imagine how this complicates things," she shared. "And the fact that Fargo's been chasing me down for some presentation to Samuel like I'm some piece of chocolate for him to handpick from the box…it's gross and I can't believe people don't see through his nasty act."

"Yeah," he murmured, still digesting her paternity bomb. "So what are you doing here? I mean, what's your plan?"

"I wanted to see for myself what this guy was all about," she said, wondering if she should tell Ford everything. It seemed smart to hold a few cards to her chest; besides, one bombshell revelation was plenty for the day, and her purpose hadn't been for her own gain, it'd been for Rafe's. "Listen, I need to talk to you about something else. What do you know about Rafe's missing baby?"

"He told you about that?" Ford asked, surprised.

"Yes," she said, drawing a deep breath to admit a little more. "Rafe and I are…close."

Ford whistled low and shook his head. "I see. All right. He's a good man, from what I can tell. You could've gotten mixed up with worse, that's for damn sure," he said. She agreed with a briefly held smile but wanted intently for Ford to answer her original question.

Ford shrugged in answer, his disappointment evident. "Not much. I heard he was asking around, asking the ladies if they'd known Abby Michaels was pregnant, but other than that…I haven't heard anything. I don't think that baby's here, to be honest."

Her hopes fell. "You don't?"

He shook his head. "No. How would you hide a baby in a town as small as this? Everyone knows everyone else's business. It's not so simple to just hide out with a kid that's not yours."

"What about this secret infirmary I've heard about?"

Ford swore under his breath. "Damn woman, talk like that could get you kicked off the island for good. I hope you haven't mentioned anything like that anywhere else. You have to be careful what falls from your mouth. Not everyone is friendly, if you know what I mean."

"I've figured that out. And you're the only one I've asked. I took a leap trusting you, but there was something about you that said I could trust you. I'm not wrong, right?"

"No. You can trust me. I don't run with that crowd. But you need to be careful making assumptions. There are a few people out there working undercover, but it's not like they're advertising a club. If asked whose side they're on, they'll likely lie for your own good and to protect their investigation. There's plenty going on that you don't need to be mixed up in, you know?"

"Thanks for the tip, but I think I can take care of myself."

"That remains to be seen." He drew a short breath. "So,

what's the doc think about you doing the Nancy Drew thing? You know this is dangerous stuff. Women have gone missing and that's a fact. I'm not saying that just to scare you."

"Like Johanna Tate?" *Like my mother?* "I know."

"Yeah, Johanna was Samuel's number-one girlfriend. And if he's willing to get rid of her, where do you think that puts you? Right in the danger zone."

"He's not going to find out about me. It's not like I'm hoping to have dinner with the man anytime soon. I just want to help Rafe find his son. Tell me about this infirmary."

"I don't know enough to tell. Just rumors and whispers. No one's really ever been there, which is why Samuel perpetuates the belief that it doesn't exist. But Doc Black is pretty sure it does."

"Do you think they might be holding his son there?"

Again, he shrugged, and his radio came to life in scratch tones and shrill whistles. He held up his hand to listen. Then he said with regret, "I hate to cut our little meeting short, but I've got to respond to that call or else Chief Fargo will have my hide. I'll give you a ride back to Doc Black's if you want."

She nodded, biting back disappointment. She'd hoped Officer McCall would have more information that could help her. It seemed he was feeling around in the dark just as much as she and Rafe were. One thing was for sure: Samuel Grayson had this town wrapped around his finger so tight, she didn't think a strand of hair could pass between the two.

Ford brought up an interesting point. If he was willing to get rid of his favorite girlfriend, what would he do to the child he'd never known about…and likely never wanted?

Chapter 18

Rafe's plan to return later that night to the clinic was moving along smoothly until he happened to bump into Dr. Bulger. The man looked tired, bags hung under his eyes and the corners of his mouth sucked in the sagging skin as discontent clearly rode him hard. Rafe felt bad for the man. Something was clearly eating at him, but he didn't know how to approach him without stepping over boundaries. He'd worked too hard to lose his position now.

Yet, even as he prepared to offer a friendly but noncommittal smile on his way out, his conscience wouldn't allow him to walk past a man in obvious need of a friend.

"Everything okay?" he asked.

Surprised at the show of concern, Rolf could only stare for a moment, then he shook his head and waved him on. "Go on. Busy day today. The clinic has more babies than we know what to do with, eh? As always, you do good work."

"Dr. Bulger…if you need anything, just ask. I'm happy to help. You seem…worn out."

Rolf bobbed a nod. "Yes, very tired. But nothing for you to worry. I'll be fine. Need just a little rest. Maybe a vacation."

"I'd be happy to fill in for you," he offered helpfully. "I wouldn't let you down."

At that Rolf eyed him with something that looked like pity mixed with regret. Rafe wondered what put the look there and why. He suspected he'd never know. He knew instinctively whatever Rolf was going through would allow for only a private audience. After a lengthy, almost uncomfortable pause, Rolf roused himself to say, shocking Rafe, "Yes…you are good man. This is not always safe place for a man such as you."

And then he turned and left the building, leaving Rafe to stare, wondering what he'd just witnessed, what the older man had just inadvertently let slip.

Or maybe it hadn't been inadvertent at all.

He was tempted to run after him, but he knew the effort would be pointless. Rolf would not share what was eating at him, and Rafe couldn't spare more time to find out.

He had a short window to get into the supply closet, before the nurses changed shifts, and hide there until the front office closed. Once closed, he could slip down the corridor that was always locked during normal hours. He'd asked about it but was told it was a wing of the clinic that hadn't been staffed yet, so it was simply empty rooms. He wanted to be sure. A copy of Rolf's key card was in his pocket, waiting for the right moment.

The minutes ticked by in agonizingly slow increments as he counted down the shift change. Finally, the time came and he eased out of the supply closet, quietly closing the door behind him. The clinic was closed, and everyone who was scheduled for the night shift at the hospital had already moved to that wing. Deathly silence rang in the halls, and shadows gathered in the darkened front office.

He waited, listening for the slightest movement, and finding total silence, he made his way to the corridor, keeping to the shadows. Sweat dampened his hairline as he approached the door blocking off the supposed empty wing. He fished the key card from his pocket and quietly slid it through the lock. The light turned from red to green and opened with a slight click. Elation beat wildly in his heart and he slipped over threshold, closing the door behind him. The halls were dimly lit, proof that this was no unfinished section of the clinic. He listened hard for movement. His ears caught a faint noise and he flattened against the wall. Someone was walking this way. He opened a side office and went inside, closing the door and waiting for the footsteps to pass. He held his breath, too afraid to breathe. What was this place? Why the secrecy? Was this the infirmary? It had to be. Why else would it be tucked behind a door that was billed as unfinished and inaccessible?

His ears pricked at a sound that stopped his heart.

An infant.

He slowly popped up and peered from the small window in the door. A nurse walked by, carrying a baby swaddled in a blue blanket. There was nothing of tenderness or caring in her body language. She neither cooed nor paid attention to the bundle in her arms. The woman might as well have been carrying a lump of dirty laundry. He watched as she cut the corner and disappeared down another corridor. Heart beating so fast he feared a cardiac event, he followed her at a safe distance. He lost sight of her for a moment, and when he turned the corner, he was met with empty halls. Panic drove him and he opened the first door to his right. He didn't have a plan if he came up face-to-face with the nurse, he just knew he had to see where she went. The baby might be his son. Why else would a baby be hidden in this dungeon, locked away? He shuddered to think that more than one child might be secreted away like this. He stared into the room, shock mingling with disappointment. A nursery of vacant cribs stared back at him, creepy and desolate in their emptiness.

Damn it. Where'd she go? And what the hell kind of nursery was this? Whose babies were put here, away from the light of normal life? Fresh agony at his failure to find his son washed over him and he couldn't help but wonder, had his son slept in this sad place? Had he been carried around by someone who saw only to his physical needs and otherwise ignored him? Was he held and cuddled? Or placed in one of these cold, impersonal cribs and left for hours at a stretch with nothing but the walls of his prison to stimulate his brain? Children needed interaction with people. The social aspect of their development was crucial. Rafe had read medical reports of children in Third-World orphanages who were never given love or affection and how it had stunted their physical and emotional growth. Some were never able to socialize ever again. It was enough to stab a fork of fear into his heart.

He turned to leave the room when he ran smack into a body. Rafe's first instinct was to run, but he stopped at the familiar scent.

Peaches and vanilla?

"Darcy?" he asked in an incredulous whisper. The woman flipped her hoodie back and grinned, albeit ruefully, as she rubbed at her chest where he'd slammed into her. Relief gave way to anger as he realized she'd followed him somehow. "What are you doing here?"

She frowned at the sharpness in his tone. "Helping you. What does it look like?"

"You shouldn't be here," he said, ignoring the flare of warmth that followed her admission. It was bad enough he was putting everything on the line; he didn't need to worry about her getting caught, too. "This is too dangerous."

"I'm not a baby and I'm not helpless," she whispered back, irritated. "Besides, I think you may want to know I think I've found a records room you might want to check out."

"Where?" he asked, instantly intrigued. He supposed the other conversation would hold, presuming they made it out of there alive. He grabbed her and placed a quick but deep kiss on her mouth. "Damn it, Darcy," he said against her lips, pulling away to stare with equal parts anger and relief. "You're the last person I want tangled up in this. I wish you would've stayed home."

"I'm not a stay-at-home kind of girl. I thought you might've noticed by now. Besides, if you're in danger, how do you think that makes me feel? I can't just sit by the sidewalk and twiddle my thumbs, hoping everything turns out all right. Forget that. I'm in. Besides, don't you like knowing someone's got your back?"

Yeah…he did. The woman had logic on her side. He bit back a grin. "Okay, but this conversation isn't over. Now, where's that records room?"

She flashed a smile and gestured. "Follow me."

Questions pounded in his brain, like how the hell had she managed to gain access to this place when it'd taken him months? But now wasn't the time to start peppering her for details. She had a point. Having someone on his side was a valuable asset. If only he wasn't worried about her in the process.

They rounded the corner and entered a room that looked like a broom closet from the outside. Once safely inside, Darcy pulled a pocket flashlight from her back jeans pocket. He was secretly impressed. Why hadn't he thought of grabbing a flashlight? Seems he was pretty pathetic in the spy department. When this was all said and done and his son was recovered, he supposed he ought to stick to what he was good at—fixing people—and leave the subterfuge to the professionals. She clicked it on and flashed the room.

"See?" She pointed to a row of file cabinets lining the wall. "I found this by accident when some nurse came my way. I had to jump in so as not to get caught. Lucky, huh?"

"Lucky that you didn't get caught," he grumbled but went to the first cabinet. He slid one open as quietly as possible, though each minute sound seemed magnified.

"I figured it ought to be something good. Why else would you keep a room in a secret clinic with files? The secret clinic alone seemed suspect. But they're not as careful as they should be," she whispered, almost conversationally, watching as Rafe flipped through files. He shot her a glance, prompting her to explain. "The sublevel basement has a window that opens right up. All I had to do was climb in, drop to the floor and then brave the creepy basement, which was daunting, I won't lie, but the lock on the door leading out is easily circumvented with a credit card. They really should be more secure in their clandestine operations."

He stifled a laugh at the irony. Here he was trying his

damndest to find a way into this place, going so far as to volunteer at the clinic just to get a copy of Rolf's key card, and Darcy had wiggled her way in like a cat burglar. Rafe shook his head. "Is this when you tell me you did time for breaking and entering when you were a kid?" he said, only slightly joking.

She punched him in the arm lightly. "Hey! I got your butt into this place. Who cares where I got my skills?"

Good point, he reasoned, continuing to flip through files, looking for names he recognized but most notably that of Abby Michaels. He stopped short, a sharp sense of apprehension following the recognition.

"Did you find something?" Darcy whispered, leaning in to see. She frowned. "Who is Liza Burbage? Someone you know?"

"A patient," he answered, pulling the file and gesturing for Darcy to hold the light so he could scan the contents. "She was diabetic and not doing well with her diet. Her insulin numbers were really unstable. I sent her to Heidi for nutrition counseling."

Darcy shuddered. "That woman would put me off from eating, that's for sure. She's like a skeleton in a skirt. And just as peppy. Why'd you send Ms. Burbage to her?"

"Samuel's orders," he said, muttering under his breath as he read. "Damn it, Liza…why is your file in here?"

Darcy looked at him, mirroring his concern. "Do you think something happened to her?"

"I don't know. She hasn't been into the office for a while. I lost track of her, to be honest. I haven't seen her around town, either. I should've followed up." Guilt ate at him, and he flipped the pages faster. "The dates stop about two weeks ago."

"You don't think…"

"I don't know what to think these days," he said grimly, tucking the file under his arm.

"What are you doing?" Darcy asked, alarmed. "You can't take that. It'll tip off that we were here, and then all hell will break loose for the both of us."

"No one is going to notice. There's hundreds of files here. Liza's isn't going to trip the radar. Besides, if something happened to her, I need proof that someone other than me saw her up until two weeks ago. Who knows, it might help prove a timeline."

"You mean, a timeline of death?" Darcy asked, her voice shaky. "That's what you mean, isn't it?"

He didn't see the sense in lying. "Yeah," he answered. "I think we should get out of here. Abby's file isn't in here and I don't want to hang around a moment longer than I have to in this place."

"Preaching to the choir. But I suggest we go out the way I came in. That way, if they research the key card, it'll look like a computer glitch."

He did a double take. "You're one smart cookie, you know that?" She flashed him a grin, though it was strained around the edges and he knew she was scared, even if she tried to hide it. He didn't blame her. They were both playing with fire. He kissed her quickly and took the lead, checking the corridor before sneaking out of the file room. His ears strained for any noise, but he was still hoping to hear a baby's cry. Maybe if he knew the direction that nurse had gone… Darcy squeezed his hand when he'd paused and stared at him in question. He shook his head, and Darcy pointed in the direction of the basement.

"First door on the right," she whispered, sticking close

to him in the milky light. "This place gives me the creeps.
I pity anyone who gets stuck here."

Rafe agreed, thinking of those empty cribs.

Especially the babies.

Chapter 19

Rolf Bulger stared into his glass of brandy, willing some kind of solace to arise from the amber liquid, yet finding none, he drained the third glass of the evening. His vision had begun to blur, but he poured another.

If solace was not to be found, he'd settle for oblivion.

If his wife, Vena, were alive, she'd likely have a few words to say about the situation, none nice or good. And he deserved a tongue-lashing. What had he been thinking?

He sighed and took a swallow, no longer wincing at the burn on his throat. "It wasn't supposed to be like this," he said to the empty room. "I never knew how it would go so badly."

Ah, Vena… His eyes watered, if from the alcohol or his blue mood, he wasn't sure, but he felt trapped in a situation without an end in sight. Damn Samuel Grayson and his foul soul, he groused as he drained the glass. He reached for another, and a noise startled him. He turned, the alcohol making his movements slow and clumsy, and seeing nothing, settled uneasily back into his chair. The brandy bottle, half-empty, remained on his birch end table, one of his wife's last purchases before she'd died in a car accident, many years ago, before he moved to Cold Plains. He smoothed his hand over the wood, feeling the grain beneath the lacquer, and wondered how far he'd get if he packed up tonight and left without saying a word. Just slipped into the night with nothing but what he could carry.

The idea held a seductive allure. Cold Plains had become a place of nightmares, not the peace and tranquility Grayson had promised.

Grayson and his lies… The man had refrained from mentioning that he was a sick bastard with a penchant for hurting young ladies…or anyone who got in his way.

Yes, leaving… The more he turned the idea in his head, the more he liked it. He struggled to rise from the deep indent he always made in his favorite chair—Vena had always harangued him to get rid of it but he'd stubbornly refused—and after he finally made it to his feet, he made an unsteady track to his bedroom to pack.

His mind was a jumbled mess, but he managed to drag his suitcase from the closet and crack it open to start throwing in whatever he could grab.

"In a rush?" a voice from the doorway said, causing him to falter and stumble against his suitcase as he turned to the sound. His heart hammered a panicked note as death stared at him with pale blue eyes. A man, dressed casually in black, leaned against the door frame of his bedroom, a smile stretching his mouth in a caricature of friendliness. "Seems you're in a hurry to go somewhere? Something wrong, Doc?"

"Who are you?" he asked, his voice pathetically weak and small. He knew not his name, but Rolf ascertained his purpose in the cold set of his jaw and eyes. This man was coming to kill him. "I've done nothing wrong," he said, trying for some semblance of bravado. "Get out before I call the chief."

The man ignored him, pushing off the door frame to invade Rolf's bedroom. The man's stare roved the room, taking in small details as if they interested him, even stopping to pick up a picture of Rolf's beloved Vena on the dresser. The man gestured to the picture. "This your old lady?" he asked, to which Rolf jerked a short nod, wanting desperately to tell this miscreant to unhand Vena's picture, but his mouth wasn't working properly. The man replaced the frame, and that was when Rolf noticed the gloves on his hands.

"You're here to kill me," Rolf stated flatly.

The man affected a wounded expression. "Doc...is that any way to start a conversation? Downright rude, if you ask me."

"Answer me, damn you," he shouted, his voice shaking. "Give me that courtesy at least."

The man spread his gloved hands in a conciliatory gesture. "I'm just here to give you a ride to wherever you were going. Would you like me to help pack your bag?" he asked, moving to the dresser. "Did you know if you roll your clothes you can actually fit more into your suitcase? I learned that on the Travel Channel. Interesting stuff on that channel." The man started to toss clothes toward Rolf, forcing him to catch them with shaking hands. He continued almost conversationally, "You know what other channel I like to watch? Animal Planet. It's full of stuff I never knew. Such as, did you know that all spiders are poisonous? Yeah, that's how they subdue their victims. Very fascinating. Can you imagine if humans could do that kind of stuff?"

Rolf couldn't stand it any longer, this cat and mouse. He threw his clothes down, shouting, "Get it over with, you sick bastard. I know that rat Grayson sent you, and I'm not afraid to die. I'll meet my maker and take my chances, but Grayson will go straight to *hell* for what he's done!" Rolf trembled from the exertion and wiped the spittle from his lip, knowing this was the end, but refusing to beg for his life.

The man stopped and faced Rolf with a hard calm. "I think you have enough for your journey. Shall we go?"

"Why this charade?" Rolf demanded, wiping at his eyes, for they had begun to leak, from tears or simply old age, he wasn't sure. His bowels felt loose, and he knew once he died what would happen. It was simple biology, but for a moment, he mourned the indignity until he realized he would be reunited with his beloved Vena when it was through. When the man simply shrugged in answer, Rolf snapped his suitcase shut and hefted it to stare at the man who awaited him.

"All set?" the man asked with false cheer. Rolf didn't dignify the question with an answer. He would not dance to Grayson's tune, not any longer, and for that he was grateful. "Excellent. I have a car waiting outside."

The man made a show of moving out of the way, and Rolf forced himself to put one foot in front of the other in stony, resigned silence.

Rolf took one last look at the little house he'd made his home since losing Vena five years ago and mentally said goodbye.

He knew he wasn't coming back.

* * *

The next morning, Rafe made a point to drive to Liza Burbage's house before work.

"How do you know where she lives?" Darcy asked.

"Small town. Besides, I checked her file. It has her address listed. I need to know she's okay."

"Does she have any family?"

"Not here in Cold Plains. I think she said she has a sister in Idaho or something like that, but she moved to Cold Plains after a painful divorce, something about having a fresh start with people who cared about her. She loved Cold Plains."

"What's not to love?" quipped Darcy. "Clear skies, clean water, maniacal narcissist running the show... Yeah, sounds like a great place to put down roots. Bring the whole fam."

Rafe shot her a look. "But on the surface, it cleans up well. What I've learned is that people who are hurting inside will overlook just about anything if they think they've found what they were searching for. From what Liza shared with me, she'd been devastated by her divorce. She came here looking for acceptance and love. Samuel seemed to offer that in spades."

"So, why'd she end up in that creepy file?"

"I can only speculate it was because of her weight."

"Samuel has it in for overweight people?"

"Samuel doesn't care for anyone with imperfections, particularly ones he feels are easily improved. Liza had a hard time sticking to her diet. She was still packing a few extra pounds."

Darcy smoothed her hand down her stomach. "I'd better lay off the cookies or the nutrition Nazi might start knocking on my door," she joked.

"You're beautiful and perfect, so you needn't worry. But Liza had age working against her. She was nearing her fifties and she couldn't seem to lay off the sweets. I was more worried about her insulin levels than her waistline, to be honest. But Samuel wanted everyone to sign off on Heidi's meal plan."

"Which, by the way," Darcy interjected with a scowl, "is total crap. For a nutritionist, she seems to take a hard and fast line against the foods that taste good. Even fruit!"

"Fruit has a lot of natural sugar," he said, pulling into Liza's driveway. Switching subjects, he noted, "Liza's car is parked here."

"Maybe she's just been hiding out," Darcy said, but there was a general dejected and forgotten air about the place that said no one had been there in weeks, and Darcy could see it as plainly as he. She exhaled, a worried frown pulling her brow. "We'd better go check it out. But I hope to God Liza Burbage is not dead in her house, because I don't think I could handle coming up on a dead body. Just giving you a heads-up that I might throw up."

"Thanks for the warning," he said, and they climbed from the car. The June heat was already promising a hot day, in spite of it being early morning. The house, like many in Cold Plains, was a bungalow style, small and compact but cute in a country way. Liza had planted spring flowers in baskets hanging from her porch, but they'd wilted from lack of water, which wasn't a good sign. Her short patch of lawn had begun to crisp, and the ground was packed hard from the heat. Not a drop of moisture had touched this place in weeks. Rafe knocked on the front door. "Liza?" he called out. "Are you in there?"

Nothing. He peered into a dusty window. Doily-dusted

furniture met his eye but no Liza. He knocked a little harder. "Liza? It's Dr. Black. Are you in there?"

"Rafe!"

Rafe bolted for the sound of Darcy's urgent call. He rounded the corner of the house and saw her cradling a limp dog, clearly near death from dehydration and hunger. "Quick, get some water," she said, distressed at the dog's condition. "Oh Rafe…he's skin and bones. How long's he been out here without any food or water?"

Rafe filled a dusty bowl with some water and rushed it over to Darcy. She helped the dog get the water to his mouth, but he was so weak she had to practically pour it down his throat. Rafe checked his collar and found a name tag. "Brando," he murmured, shaking his head. "Figures. Liza was a huge Marlon Brando fan. Damn it," he said, rubbing the dog's flank, knowing for certain Liza would never have left her beloved dog behind.

"Did you know she had a dog?" Darcy asked.

"No… I mean, she talked about someone named Brando, but I always assumed it was a friend…not a dog."

"The poor thing," Darcy murmured, giving Brando a few more tries at the water. Brando whined, a sad, pathetic sound if Rafe had ever heard one, and then laid his head back in Darcy's lap. Darcy didn't seem to care that she was sitting in the dirt with someone else's nearly dead mutt in her arms. In that instance, he saw Darcy's strength of character, and his heart gave in just a little bit more.

"I'm going to see if I can find a blanket for him to lie on in the car," Rafe said, jogging away to look. He made another circle of the house and found a folded blanket on the porch, near a well-worn chair he supposed Liza used to stargaze, another one of her hobbies she didn't mind sharing with Rafe on her patient visits. He had a bad feeling about all this. *Damn you, Grayson,* he thought mutinously. *Rotten son-of-a-bitch...* He'd better get what was coming to him soon, or Rafe didn't know if he could keep himself in check much longer, and he could end up blowing this whole operation with one well-timed punch to the jaw.

"What are we going to do with him?" Darcy asked, once they were in the car. The dog, a medium-size breed of indeterminate lineage, remained in Darcy's lap, in spite of his suggestion to put him in the backseat. "We can't just take him to the pound. After all he's been through, that would be insult to injury."

"He needs a vet," Rafe said, glancing at the dog, doubtful he would even make it through the night. "But he looks pretty bad. We don't know how long he went without water."

"Let's go straight to the vet's office, then," Darcy said resolutely. "I'm not going to rest until I know this little guy has been taken care of."

Rafe bit back a sigh. Taking responsibility for an orphaned animal wasn't high on his priority list, but when he saw Darcy caring so deeply for this poor, forgotten mutt, he softened. How could he say no when he'd also benefited from Darcy's generous nature? If it hadn't been for her, he'd still be stumbling around in the dark of that secret clinic, likely getting stuck in a broom closet. "We'll take him to the vet's before we head to the office. They'll take good care of him there," he assured Darcy, smiling when some of the tension left Darcy's body.

A moment of silence followed, until Darcy, stroking Brando's matted fur, said quietly, "You know it's probably likely that Liza is dead. I don't think she'd leave behind her dog. There's too much evidence that she loved this dog. His collar is monogrammed and so was his food and water bowl. That's not someone who doesn't give a rip about their animal."

"I know," he agreed, hating the obvious conclusion. "I'll go to the police station and report her missing. Maybe someone's heard something."

"Don't go to Fargo. Tell officer McCall. He'll care."

He looked at her sharply, but Darcy's attention was focused on the dog. How well did she know McCall? Her tone suggested a familiarity that struck him as odd. It wasn't jealousy, he told himself. It was something else. Something else entirely. But it sure felt like the stirrings of jealousy.

Yeah, keep telling yourself that, buddy.

His jaw tensed at his own ridiculous mental babbling and he focused on the road. He had bigger problems.

Darcy worried as she worked. Her thoughts kept circling back to the dog and what might've happened to Liza. Her disappearance made the danger that much more real. This wasn't a game. There were real lives at stake. It sobered her quickly. It wasn't that she'd underestimated the danger, but there had been a sense of intrigue that hadn't felt entirely real. Maybe she *had* underestimated the danger level. She suppressed a shudder. Suddenly, she felt a lot more vulnerable than before. Until Louise, death had never been a part of her landscape. She hadn't known anyone who'd died, and when Louise had been taken from her so suddenly, Darcy had been in a state of denial. Maybe that's what this trip was, a method to push away her true grief. A wild adventure filled with mystery and intrigue while she ferreted out the particulars of her biological mother's life with this *supposedly* dangerous man.

But that's where it got real. Samuel Grayson *was* a dangerous man. And he might very well have killed her biological mother. It put things in perspective in a way that hadn't been clear before. It was as if a haze had been lifted from her vision, and the picture she saw scared the socks from her feet.

Maybe she ought to cut her losses and leave. That would be the smart thing to do, but what about Rafe? She couldn't leave him behind. And he wasn't leaving without his son. Not that she blamed him. He had a very good reason to stay.

Rafe's patient said her goodbyes, and then Rafe appeared, framed in the hallway. "Did you talk to McCall?" she asked.

"Not yet. I'm going to go there after the clinic closes." He rubbed his hands together, deep in thought, as if wrestling with something. Then he said, "How do you know McCall?"

She stopped, wondering how much to tell. In hindsight, carjacking an officer she hadn't known very well seemed very foolish, and she really didn't want to admit her folly to Rafe. But she also felt a bit of guilt for sharing her secret with McCall when she hadn't managed to tell the man she was falling in love with and, oh, incidentally, sleeping with every night. She fretted for a moment as a second thought came to her. Would McCall tell Rafe about her paternity? Even as she considered the possibility, her instinct told her McCall wouldn't. She might be off base, but she had to trust in something and she chose to trust in McCall's silence.

"I met him in the library, remember? I told you about

that," she said, hoping that was true. "He introduced himself to me when I was doing research. He seemed nice and not crazy like the rest of the Grayson disciples." She shrugged it off. "Why?"

"No reason. Just curious," he said, backing away. "My next patient should be here soon. I'll be back in a second."

"Okay," she said, watching quizzically as he excused himself. That man was an irritatingly deep well. She dialed the vet's office to check on Brando for the third time that hour. She didn't care if they were tired of taking her calls. For some reason, that dog meant something to her and she couldn't fathom the thought of him dying.

And it gave her something else to focus on rather than the reality of what she'd willingly put herself into.

Chapter 20

By the end of the day, Rafe could tell something was eating at Darcy but she wouldn't share, so he opted to give her space. It wasn't his first choice, but apart from sitting her down and coaxing the issue out of her, his options were slim. While Darcy went to check on Brando the dog, Rafe went to report Liza missing.

He walked into the station hoping to find McCall but got Chief Fargo instead.

"What can I do you for, Doc?" Fargo asked around his shredded toothpick.

"I'm here to report a missing person," he answered, hiding his hatred for the man behind a mask of professionalism. Rafe knew of Fargo's dirtier deeds since Brenda Billings was one of his patients. He'd seen the bruises and the look of fear when Fargo was around. In Rafe's eyes, Fargo was no different than Samuel. Fargo, at the very least, didn't pretend to be anything other than what he was—a self-serving prick. Rafe supposed he could give him credit for that, but only grudgingly so.

Fargo's brow went up as he leaned forward in interest. "Who?"

"One of my patients, Liza Burbage?"

Fargo searched his memory, then squinted in memory. "That the fat older gal?"

Rafe's mouth seamed shut for fear of telling Fargo to go screw himself and to get off his high horse. Fargo wasn't exactly svelte these days. It was a wonder Samuel didn't have his favored pet on a diet, as well. But Rafe supposed that when you were the number-one whore for the man running the show, you can get away with a lot that others can't. Rafe ignored Fargo's insult and continued, saying, "She was a type 2 diabetic. I hadn't seen her in a while and I went to her house to check on her and found the place empty, plants and dog nearly dead."

"A dog?" Fargo repeated, something in his expression. "What kind?"

"One that was her heart and soul, which is why I know she wouldn't have left him behind. Something is wrong."

"I'm sure it's nothing. Probably got tired of taking care of the mutt and just took off. It happens."

Rafe counted to ten mentally. "Maybe. But not with Liza. She wasn't that kind of person. It's safe to say I knew her fairly well as my patient. She wouldn't have left without that dog, and I'd appreciate it if you'd file a missing-person report."

The note of steel in his voice caught Fargo's attention, and the cop's stare narrowed, but he didn't take the bait. Fargo must've realized to ignore Rafe's concerns would be to cause undue attention on his practices, but even as he went to grab the necessary paperwork, it wasn't done with any sense of grace. "Give me the details and I'll put it out there. But I'm telling you right now, she probably just left."

Oh, she left, all right, in a garbage bag, most likely, Rafe wanted to mutter but forced a perfunctory smile. "And there's something else I want to talk to you about," Rafe ventured, feeling a bit reckless in the face of Fargo's blatant laziness. He was tired of being cautious, patiently waiting for word he knew wasn't coming unless he prodded the man. "I want to know if there's been any movement on my son's case?"

Fargo barely looked up from the paperwork as he said, "No. I'll call you if there is."

"What will it take to put more resources on this case?"

"Look, Doc, I sympathize with your situation, but frankly, there's the feeling that you're barking up the wrong tree. No one remembered this Abby chick being pregnant. And even if she was, you don't even know if it's yours. Do you have a paternity test, something in writing that says the kid is yours?"

"No, but I know," Rafe said, refusing to let Fargo think he'd swept away his conviction. "He's mine. And his name is Devin."

"And what makes you so sure?" Fargo asked, irritated.

"I have a picture of him and he is my spitting image," Rafe said hotly, unable to keep his temper in check.

"A picture? Where'd you get a picture?"

Rafe saw no reason to lie. "Abby sent it to me."

Fargo's mouth tensed for a moment, but then he shrugged. "Well, all babies tend to look like the other, so who knows if that picture is even your kid? Listen, I hear you, you're all fired up and I've put as much resources as I can into this case. But to be frank, it's not going anywhere without more evidence. It is what it is. Maybe it's time to move on."

"Move on?" he repeated incredulously. "You don't move on from your children."

"To be fair, you never even met the kid."

"Chief…you have no clue what you're talking about," Rafe said, taking great effort not to curl his hands into fists. But even so, his voice was cold enough to burn as he said, leaning forward to make his point clear, "Listen up, Chief. Here's the deal. I'm not giving up. I will tear this town down if I have to to find my son. All I want is my son. That's it. He's mine and I want him. Plain and simple. I won't give up. I won't forget. Am I clear?"

Rafe was taking a chance—a desperate, bold and possibly stupid chance—but he'd reached his limit. The knowledge of those empty cribs lingered in his memory, spurring him to make a move, even if it was a foolish one. Desperate men made desperate choices and he fully recognized himself as one of those men, but he couldn't waste another minute standing idly by while his son was possibly treated as an "it." God only knew what was happening to those kids. He shuddered to think…

Fargo tried staring him down, but Rafe met him stare for stare, almost daring him to push. Fargo sensed a difference in Rafe and, ever the calculating man, dialed it down a bit with a mollifying gesture. "Calm down, Doc. You're distraught. I want to help you out, I do. Sorry if that didn't come across. How about this… Bring me that picture and I'll post a bulletin. How's that?"

"It's a start," Rafe said, his adrenaline still racing. He took a moment to compose himself. "Thank you, Chief. I'll bring it first thing tomorrow morning."

"Good." Fargo took a breath. "Now is there anything else I can help you with?"

"That's it."

"Great. Easily done. Now before you go, I have a favor to ask of you. You help me, I help you. That's the Cold Plains way, right?"

Rafe choked back the bile. "What do you need?"

Fargo lost some of his fake cheer. "That little lady that works for you. Mr. Grayson has taken quite a shine to her. Maybe you can convince her to stop by and say hello." It wasn't a question, it was a demand, and Rafe was under no illusion that it was otherwise. "That would be right kind of you. I've had a difficult time catching her. You keep her pretty busy, Doc."

"I'll save you the effort, Chief," Rafe said. "She's unavailable. She's with me."

Fargo's jaw tightened, and the toothpick in his mouth stilled. "Come again?"

"She and I are dating. Darcy is unavailable."

"My, my, Doc. You're a wily one, aren't you? Can't say I blame you. She's a hot piece of tail."

Fargo was trying to get a rise out of him. Rafe simply held his tongue and shrugged. "She's a good person. We have a lot in common."

"I guess so. Well, Mr. Grayson will certainly be disappointed."

"I'm sure he'll recover. He has plenty of young ladies just waiting to make his acquaintance."

"True. But he really had his eye on Darcy."

Rafe used Fargo's words against him, saying, "It is what it is, right?"

"Yeah…I guess it is."

"I'll bring the picture in tomorrow," Rafe said, ready to

end this conversation before someone went too far. He'd likely already bought himself a one-way ticket to somewhere bad in Fargo's book, but he couldn't restrain himself, not this time.

"You do that," Fargo said, removing the toothpick and tossing it in the trash beside his desk. "See you around, Doc."

Rafe nodded and split. One more second in that man's company, and Rafe didn't think he could hold back.

He might've already screwed the pooch, but it was time for action—one way or another.

Fargo's gut churned. So the doc was nailing his pretty receptionist. Figures. Seems he wasn't so high-and-mighty, after all. But that presented an ugly problem for him with Grayson. He'd become obsessed with having Darcy, and no one else seemed to appease his appetite. So where'd that leave Fargo? Between a rock and a hard place.

Maybe it was time for Darcy to leave town. If she wasn't here to tempt or taunt Grayson, then maybe Grayson would lose interest and turn his eye elsewhere.

It was definitely food for thought.

Now for the bigger issue. Doc Black wasn't giving up on that brat of his. Where the hell had a picture come from? That complicated matters. If Black chose to take this to a higher level, it could raise some uncomfortable questions for Grayson, which in turn would make his life miserable.

He leaned back in his chair, listening as the leather squealed in protest. Fargo rubbed his belly, wincing at the acid reflux splashing up his windpipe. He needed a vacation, one free from all the drama that dogged him here in Cold Plains. Or maybe he just needed to release some tension. He considered his options for a moment, then grabbed his cell phone. He texted Brenda, his favorite girl, their code. Maybe he'd marry Brenda. He liked her well enough. Liked screwing her, that was for sure. She was quiet, demure and knew how to keep her mouth shut. In modern days such as these, that was a golden quality. Marrying Brenda would give him an air of respectability, which he seemed to lack. He pictured her round eyes, the way she flinched when he raised his hand against her and the way she groaned when he was pounding into her petite body with his bulk. Yes, a visit to Brenda would ease the tension and then he could fix this Doc Black situation, which was a pain in his side.

With a plan in place, Fargo popped four antacids and happily headed out the door.

Samuel paced his secret conference room, angry. Darcy was with Dr. Black? How'd that happen? Was he losing his touch? What happened to the women who fell at his feet, eager to please him? Panic ate at his normal confidence, that self-assured quality that had gained him an empire, and he had to force himself to calm. This was a momentary setback, not a harbinger of doom.

One fickle woman was not a trustworthy gauge of his popularity, he told himself, smoothing his shirt of imaginary wrinkles.

However, it did add validity to that quack Bulger's claim that he'd pushed a little hard. He had to remind people that he was there for them and only interested in the community's health and welfare. Without those platitudes armoring him on all sides, he was left vulnerable to those who sought to take him down.

People like that damn Officer McCall. Oh, there were

others, hiding behind their false smiles and pretend support, but McCall was being the biggest pain in his ass.

Damn you, Johanna. Faithless bitch. It was her fault he had the FBI sniffing around his back door, trying to gain entrance into his sanctuary. If McCall hadn't convinced Eden Police that the FBI lab ought to test the forensics on Johanna's body, this whole sordid mess would have remained a bad memory.

He growled, his body tensing. No one crossed him and lived to tell. Maybe he ought to teach that young cop a lesson on who runs this town.

Calm yourself, a voice in his head cautioned. *Rash decisions cause costly mistakes.* True, he agreed. He'd been living fast and loose too much lately. Time to rein it in. No more playing. Time to work.

Samuel closed his eyes, drew a deep breath and exhaled slowly. After a few more times, the anger receded and he was able to think clearly.

Which, given this current situation with Dr. Black and his missing brat, was a very good thing, indeed.

Seems he'd underestimated the good doctor's resilience and dedication. He had two choices: one choice would create a sworn enemy; the other would possibly create an ally.

The choice was simple, really.

But how to execute was the question....

Chapter 21

"How'd it go over at the police station?" Darcy asked, once they were in the car. "Did you talk to McCall?"

"He wasn't available. I had to talk to the chief," Rafe answered, his eyes never leaving the road. Something was bugging him, something that happened at the station. She didn't want to pry since that would have been the height of hypocrisy when she'd shut him out all day from her own private struggles. But she sensed whatever it was, was big. "How's the dog?" he asked.

It was polite interest, not genuine concern, Darcy knew, but she appreciated the effort. "Good. He needs to stay a few nights, but the veterinarian seems to think he'll pull through, and the vet has agreed to adopt him himself. He took one look at Brando and said he reminded him of a dog he'd had as a kid. He was very dehydrated, but not as bad as we'd thought. The vet estimated that he'd been without water for about four days."

"Four days?" Rafe seemed troubled. "But Liza's been gone at least two weeks. That doesn't seem to add up. Do you think someone, maybe a neighbor, has been bringing the dog food and water?"

"I don't know. There weren't too many neighbors that I could see," Darcy said, dubious. "Probably the dog was drinking whatever was left over from when Liza disappeared. It was a pretty deep water dish."

"Yeah, that makes sense. So a few more days?" he asked, no doubt picturing the monstrous bill that would come home.

"I'll pay for his vet bill," she offered, feeling slightly guilty for thrusting this new development on Rafe, but what could she do? Darcy had always had a soft spot for animals and couldn't imagine just turning the pooch over to the pound for an uncertain future given what he'd already been through.

He flashed a brief smile and reached over to rub her knee. "It's okay. I can handle the vet bill. I'm just glad he's going to be all right, and that he's found a good home."

"Really? Are you sure?" she asked, her guilt still nagging at her. Or maybe it wasn't just guilt about the dog. "I feel bad," she admitted.

"Bad? Why?"

She shrugged. "I sort of bulldozed you into this position with the dog. The least I can do is pay for the bill."

He chuckled. "You didn't bulldoze me," he assured her. "I was worried about the dog, too. Besides, Liza would want someone looking after Brando, and Liza was a good patient. I don't mind helping out."

She smiled, warmth spreading in her chest. Rafe was such a good man. Anyone who would shoulder the burden he was carrying and yet had strength enough to add a homeless orphaned dog was a champion in her book. Darcy reached over and caressed the back of his neck, secretly basking in the love she felt for this man. And yet something sat between them, her secret.

Her instinct told her Rafe wouldn't hold it against her that Samuel was her father. However, he might be hurt that she'd withheld that information this long from him yet had freely told Ford McCall. Was it like pulling off a bandage? A quick rip was far better than a tentative pull? Should she just come out and level with Rafe and let the chips fall where they may? Logic said, yes. But her heart screamed, *Are you crazy? It's too big of a risk!*

"You're quiet all of a sudden," Rafe remarked. "Everything okay?"

"No," she answered, biting her lip. "But I'm not ready to talk about it."

"That's a cryptic answer."

"Sorry. It's all I've got." She sighed, hating how she sounded. She'd never been the type of woman to play coy games but she knew that was how she came off at the moment. "It's something personal and I'm trying to decide the best way to handle it," she said, trying to smooth over the rough edges of her previous statement. "I know that's not a fair answer, but I promise I will tell you when I think it's time."

"Now you've got me worried," Rafe said, his brow furrowing. "Maybe if you talked it out, you'd find the answer more quickly. I'm a good listener."

"I know you are. The problem isn't you, it's me." He cast her a semiplayful look and she chuckled at her choice of words. "I know, that's a classic relationship line that's been used in countless movies and books, but in this instance, it's true."

"Okay," he allowed, backing off to give her the space she needed and desperately appreciated. "I'm here if you need me."

"Thanks."

"Hey, I should tell you something else that happened at the station," he said, switching tracks, for which she was absurdly grateful. "I told Fargo I wanted more resources put on my son's case and that you and I were together."

"Whoa. Back it up. Those are two bombshells. First, how'd he take the demand for more resources?" she asked.

"Not well, but in the end, he saw things my way. He's agreed to post a bulletin with Devin's picture tomorrow. I just have to bring him the photo."

"Funny how he never offered to do that before," Darcy said, not trusting that creepy chief farther than she could throw him. "Don't you find his sudden helpfulness suspect?"

"Of course, but he didn't come to this newfound helpfulness without a little prodding on my part."

"Well, whatever you did, I hope it works."

"Me, too."

"And how did he take the news that you and I were an item?"

"Worse than the other. He looked mad enough to chew nails, which tells me that Samuel's been putting serious pressure on Fargo to get you to play ball."

Darcy shuddered. It was a Greek tragedy just waiting to happen. Good gravy, the idea was…simply appalling. "Well, maybe he'll lay off and leave me alone now."

"Maybe. Let's hope."

They finished the ride to the house in silence, each locked in their own thoughts. Darcy appreciated that Rafe had claimed her as his own, but she couldn't help but wonder if that might backfire on them both. From what she'd learned thus far of Samuel, he didn't take setbacks lightly and he really didn't handle jealousy well.

A part of her wondered just how shocked Samuel would be and what he would do if she came out and said, "Hey, Samuel, sorry I've been ducking you and ruining your little plan for seduction, but here's the thing—I'm your daughter."

What made her equally sick to her stomach was the chance that Samuel might find the idea of sleeping with his own daughter intriguing. As twisted as he was…she couldn't discount the possibility.

The next morning, Rafe went to grab his photo of Devin and found it missing.

"Darcy!" he called out, dread rising in his voice. "Have you seen my picture of Devin?"

Darcy appeared, drying her hair. "I thought you kept it in your wallet?"

"I did, but I took it out a few days ago because I planned to scan it into my hard drive so I would have more than one copy. I put it here on the desk."

She responded with a solemn shake of her head and apprehension in her eyes. "No, Rafe. I haven't seen it."

"It was right here," he said, more to himself than anyone else. He started shoving papers aside and tearing open drawers. *"Right here!"* He swore. "How could I be so stupid?"

"You think someone took it?"

"Damn straight, I think someone took it. It was the one piece of evidence I had of Devin being real when everyone in this godforsaken town has been trying to convince me that he doesn't exist." Angry tears pricked his eyes and he ground them out with the heel of his palm. That corpulent bastard Fargo got someone to come into his house when he and Darcy were gone and snatched it. And Rafe had made it damn easy for him, too, by keeping it in plain sight. Rafe was sick to his stomach. He wanted to storm into that police station and shake the information out of Fargo, but he knew that would likely get him shot, and probably just the thing Fargo would love to do so he could claim self-defense. He had to throttle it back before he lost his mind. "Darcy, please call my patients and reschedule. I'm taking a personal day," he said before stalking from the house. He needed to run, to clear his head, or else he was going to do something crazy.

Darcy stared as Rafe left the house in a black rage. She didn't begrudge him the freak-out, but seeing him so lost was unsettling. The knowledge that someone had invaded their home made her feel vulnerable. She glanced around the familiar surroundings and wondered where they'd gained entry. Instead of standing around being scared, Darcy was propelled to do something. She went around the house and checked every possible door and window, looking for a sign of forced entry. She checked the front door and found nothing, not that she expected to—most thieves don't walk up to the front door, brazen as you please, and kick it in. But she checked it anyway, looking for tool marks. Then she did the same for every door in the house. She went to the garage and found the doorjamb splintered. Darcy swore under her breath. She'd watched on a police program how the garage door was the most vulnerable as it usually only had a flimsy lock to the outside and was made of cheap wood. A person could practically put their foot through the door if they had enough force. But all it takes is a good kick, and it'll splinter the jamb, which is what had happened.

And because the garage door had been locked, they hadn't bothered to lock the door leading into the house.

It'd been foolish and she felt partly responsible. But she supposed placing blame wasn't going to help, so she simply prepared to be as supportive as possible when Rafe returned. In the meantime, she had phone calls to make.

By midafternoon, Rafe had found some semblance of calm, though a lake of red-hot anger seethed beneath a thin, barely there surface. When his cell phone rang, he was tempted to ignore it, but when he glanced at the caller ID and saw that it was Virgil Cruthers, his good sense prevailed and he took the call.

"Playing hooky today, I see," Virgil said with good-natured humor. Unfortunately Rafe couldn't find it in him to banter. Not today.

"How can I help you, Virgil?" he inquired politely.

Sensing Rafe wasn't in the mood to joke, Virgil got straight to the point. "How would you be interested in heading the OB department in the clinic?" he asked, shocking Rafe into stunned silence.

When he found his voice, he said, "What about Dr. Bulger?"

"Rolf is no longer with us. He decided to retire to Florida."

"That seems sudden. I just talked to him. He never said anything about retiring to Florida."

"Yes, well, who knows what was going through the mind of that crazy Hungarian. Anyway, it's a done deal. He's gone and we need someone with experience. You seem to be working out well at the clinic and we'd love to have you. Of course, we'd have to discuss fair compensation because you wouldn't have time to operate your practice."

This was all too much to take in. He needed time to process. "Virgil, I'm flattered, but I'm going to need to think about it. Can you give me a few days?"

"Of course, but don't take too long. Opportunities like this don't fall out of the sky."

No, they happened when someone disappeared, creating an opening. "Thanks, Virgil."

"You bet. I look forward to nailing down the specifics," Virgil said as if Rafe's acceptance was a foregone conclusion. Before Rafe could clarify his position, Virgil had hung up.

"What was that all about?" Darcy asked.

"I was just offered a job as head of the OB department at the clinic," Rafe said, pocketing his cell. "Dr. Bulger retired to Florida, suddenly."

Darcy stared. "Florida? Maybe that's where Liza went, too. Seems a nice way of putting murder."

"We don't know if they're dead," he reminded her, but the admonition rang hollow. He didn't hold much hope that Liza was alive, and now, hearing about Bulger, he didn't have a good feeling about the older Hungarian, either. "The last time I saw him, something was bothering him, but he wouldn't talk about it."

Darcy exhaled, shaking her head. "People are disappearing at a rapid rate around here. Maybe we ought to get the hell out while we still can."

He looked at her sharply. "Not without my son."

She nodded, almost miserably. "I know. It was just a thought."

"You should go," he said, looking away. "But I'm not going anywhere."

"I'm just saying you're not going to be much good to Devin if you're dead, and it seems people who piss off Samuel Grayson end up six feet under somewhere, *vacationing* in Florida."

"If they were going to do something, they would've done it by now. Besides, they wouldn't offer me a job at the clinic without plans to keep me around for a while."

"Don't take that job," Darcy said, her tone urgent. "I have a really bad feeling about it."

"It would be a perfect opportunity for me to get in on the inside," he countered, ignoring that little voice that sided with Darcy. "No more skulking around in broom closets—I would have easy access and cause to be there. No one would question if I was walking around, because I'd have clearance."

"And you think that clearance wouldn't come at a price?" she asked, tears sparkling in her eyes. "I'm serious, Rafe. This is a devil's bargain. They know you're onto them, and what better way to keep an eye on you than to rope you into something you can't get out of? You might start on the right side, but in no time at all you'll be sliding down a slippery slope. What do you think all those cribs are for?" He startled, unaware that she'd seen the cribs that night. She nodded vigorously. "Yeah, I saw them. And you and I both know nothing good was happening to those babies. What if you're asked to do something you're morally against but can't get out of? This is bad. *Very bad.* And the very fact that Samuel has his greasy fingers all over it should tell you to steer clear."

All salient points. But there was a seductive quality to the offer that was hard to ignore. "I have to make the choice that's right for my son," he said, stubbornly clinging to the idea that being on the inside might bring him closer to the truth. "I know it's hard for you to understand—"

"You're damn straight it's hard for me to understand, because you're being a jackass," she interrupted hotly, wiping away the tears that had begun to track down her cheeks. "I just lost my mother. I'm not about to lose someone else I love just because they wanted to play the hero."

Rafe stared, stunned, as Darcy spun on her heel and disappeared into her own bedroom, slamming the door and keeping him out.

She loved him?

She loved him.

Ah hell...this complicated things.

Because he loved her, too.

Chapter 22

Darcy spent a restless night in a cold double bed in the guest room, the room that was supposed to be for her, yet she'd never slept in once. Her bed had been with Rafe, always.

She rose when the sun crested the horizon, eager to be free from that lonely bed, and quickly showered and got ready to head to the office. She was ashamed of how she'd behaved last night, wishing she'd shown more maturity, but it scared her to irrationality to think that Rafe might be willfully putting himself in danger. She wanted him to find his son, but she didn't want to lose Rafe in the process.

And there was still the issue sitting between them that Rafe wasn't even aware of: her paternity. She worried her bottom lip, rehearsing in her head a few possible scenarios where she spilled the beans, and his subsequent—possible—reactions. Best-case scenario, he laughed at her fears and told her he didn't care who had fathered her; worst-case scenario, he looked at her with disgust and kicked her out of his home and his life. Surely there was a happy medium somewhere between those two scenarios…. She swallowed and kissed her pendant for luck, figuring she needed all that she could get.

Rafe was waiting for her with a coffee mug in hand, a peace offering if there ever was one, and she accepted it wordlessly. She didn't trust her voice right now; she was too close to tears as it was.

"Good morning," he murmured, ducking down to kiss her sweetly. "I missed you."

She stared up at him, the coffee mug between them, and jerked a short nod. "Yeah, me, too. I mean, I missed you, too."

"Are we still fighting?" he asked.

"Are you still considering that job offer at the clinic?" Rafe's mouth tightened and she had her answer. She blinked back tears. "We'd better get to the office. Your patients will be arriving soon."

"Darcy…"

She waved away his protests, not interested in rehashing the argument if neither of their positions had changed. "Hurry. We'll be late. I need to check on Brando before we open."

Rafe nodded, plainly not satisfied with her answer, but at least he respected her wishes.

Rafe felt like a jerk. He'd caused those tears glittering in Darcy's eyes, and it made him sick. But how could he pass up this opportunity to get in on the inside of that place, when his son might be hidden there? Didn't she understand he'd do anything to get his son back? Even sacrifice his morality? His dignity? His relationship with Darcy?

No. He talked a good game, but when he thought of losing Darcy, a sharp pain in his chest followed. In a very short time, she'd become an integral part of him.

Did Darcy have a point about his taking that job? He knew in his heart that Rolf Bulger was not vacationing in Florida, and yet he was considering eagerly sliding into the man's position. What had Bulger done to piss off Samuel, and for that matter, how long would it take before Rafe made the same mistake? Likely not long, seeing as his objective had nothing to do with Samuel's agenda and everything to do with his own. One thing was for certain: anyone who played for Samuel Grayson's team gave up something—likely their souls—and there was no backing out. He wasn't willing to play by Grayson's rules. Deep in his heart, he knew he couldn't.

So, that left only one option.

And Darcy had known all along. Too bad he'd been too stubborn to see what had been right in front of him.

An odd queasiness gripped Darcy's stomach, and for an agonizing moment, she thought she might throw up. It was the stress, she reasoned, reaching into her purse for some gum. Nothing more.

But then another wave of nausea washed over her and she looked to her calendar with apprehension.

No... she thought. *One time without a condom?* How could it be that easy? But the calendar dates stared at her without pity. She should've started her period a week ago.

Are you kidding me? On top of everything else, a pregnancy scare?

What would Rafe say? She bit her fingernail absently

until she heard her mother's voice in her head telling her to stop. She dropped her hand to her lap and smoothed her blouse over her stomach. Could she have Rafe's baby growing inside her? A little piece of Rafe and her, blending into one perfect package? She startled at the weepy maternal streak, which she'd never felt before in her life. She hadn't wanted kids. She certainly hadn't ever cooed or gushed over other people's babies. What kind of mother would she make? She already knew Rafe would be an excellent father. But as to her skills…she was already scared for the kid. She didn't know how to change a diaper or even what to feed a kid aside from breast milk, but what after that? And breast-feeding? She touched her breasts lightly, searching for any telltale tenderness or fullness that hadn't been there before. How could she manage a kid chewing on her nipples like one of those monkeys in the wild? She shuddered and then felt ashamed for her selfishness. Of course she would breast-feed. It made kids smarter, right?

"Darcy?" Rafe's voice cut into her rambling thoughts and she actually jumped, nearly falling from her chair. "Are you all right?" he asked, concerned. "You look a little pale. Do you need anything?"

"Why would you ask that?" she asked, her eyes wide. Did he know? He was a doctor; maybe he could see some kind of universal, biological, neon signs that she'd completely missed. "I'm fine. Really. Fine. Perfectly so. And definitely not queasy or light-headed."

He stared at her oddly, no doubt wondering if she'd fallen and bumped her head.

Darcy stood and shouldered her purse. "I'm going out for some lunch. Should I pick you up something?"

"Whatever would be fine," he said, not convinced. "Are you sure—"

"Positive." Oh! She reddened and moved away from him, darting for the door. "I'll be back. Bye!"

If there were an award for acting conspicuous, she would've been a nominee if not the winner. But her head was a tangled mess. She couldn't be pregnant. She wasn't ready. Rafe certainly didn't need this sort of added complication in his life. It wasn't fair to either of them.

And it wasn't fair to Devin, either. The poor kid hadn't even met his father yet and he might be getting a sibling. She groaned. Hells bells, how'd this happen?

She stepped off the curb, intent to duck into the coffee shop for a Danish or something else sweet, when the air was knocked from her lungs as she fell to the ground, skinning her palms. She'd definitely been shoved, she thought in shock, turning to see who had been so rude, when a nondescript car barreled past her, missing her by inches. The car sped off down Main Street and disappeared without stopping to see if she was all right.

She sucked in a gasping breath, realizing that being short of breath was a small price to pay for being alive. That car could've killed her. Cold fear washed over her even as she tried to appear unaffected by the brush of death disguised as an ugly sedan.

"Are you okay?" She heard Rafe's voice, realizing it was him who'd knocked her out of harm's way. She turned and found Rafe staring at her, fear in his expression. She managed a nod but winced as she struggled to sit up. A crowd had begun to gather and her cheeks burned uncomfortably.

"Is she all right, Dr. Black?"

"Did you see how fast that car was traveling?"

"Did anyone catch the license plate? I've never seen that car in town before."

"Must be an out-of-towner…"

The questions and comments coming at her were nearly overwhelming and she clung to Rafe. "Just get me out of here," she murmured and Rafe understood.

"Let's give her some room, people," he instructed firmly, and a path cleared for them. Rafe thanked everyone for their concern and led Darcy to a private spot in the park across from the library.

"How'd you know?" Darcy stared, amazed. "If it wasn't for you, I'd be roadkill."

"You were acting so strangely I followed you with the intent to catch lunch together. I could tell you were distracted, because you never even heard me calling your name. You stepped off the curb, and that car came out of nowhere. Darcy, I think it wasn't an accident."

Darcy's mouth gaped slightly, though a part of her may have suspected it. As far as she'd seen thus far, no one in town drove faster than a person could walk briskly, and whoever was driving that sedan had been trying to qualify for NASCAR. Someone had tried to…kill her? Even with the evidence staring her in the face, it was hard to fully comprehend. In all of her life, she'd never been threatened. It was a sobering thought, one that created troubling questions. "No…it had to be an accident. Who would try to kill me in broad daylight?"

"Someone who didn't have cause to worry he'd get caught," Rafe said grimly. "Plus, if pressed, it could've looked like an accident."

She shuddered and Rafe wrapped her in a tight hug. "Darcy, when I thought that car was going to hit you, everything became very clear. I'm not going to take that job.

You were right. It is a devil's bargain. I'll find Devin a different way."

Tears brimmed in her eyes and she wiped them away, but they came harder. Too many secrets in this damn place. Including her own. She couldn't take it any longer. If she was going to die, it was going to be with a clear conscience.

He gently pulled her hands free from her face. "What's wrong?" he asked.

"I...I have something to tell you," she said, wiping her nose. "And you're not going to like it."

He drew back, and the apprehension in his expression caused that queasy feeling to return to her gut. "What is it?"

"I...well, I..." *Just say it already.* She drew a halting breath. "I'm actually Samuel Grayson's daughter."

Rafe stared. "What?"

She sobbed harder, nodding as if she knew this admission was a death sentence. "I just found out recently and I came here because my biological mother may have been murdered by Samuel and I thought if I came here I could find answers, but I found you instead and I never thought I'd come here and fall in love but I did and now I'm afraid that you'll hate me because I've been tainted by my father's DNA."

It was a lot to take in. The questions started almost immediately, but for a moment, he had to digest everything. His silence provoked a more earnest explanation from Darcy, which saved him the effort of asking the questions.

"My mother, Louise, died of cancer, but before she died she dropped a bombshell on me, admitting that she wasn't my biological mother. My mother, her name was Catherine, gave me to Louise with an ardent plea to keep me safe and away from Samuel. Louise was worried that my ignorance might hurt me in the long run and so she shared the secret she'd been carrying my entire life. I came here looking for answers, but I've come up nearly as empty as you've come up with Devin."

"I see," he murmured, still a bit shell-shocked.

"Do you feel differently about me?" she asked fearfully and he realized she mistook his silence for one of condemnation. He sighed and wrapped her in his arms. How could she think that he could stop loving her over something out of her control? She shuddered in relief, crying soft mewling little cries. "I thought for sure you'd hate me after I told you. McCall told me I should just tell you—"

He stilled. McCall? He pulled away. "You told McCall? But not me?"

She faltered, as if realizing she probably should've kept that to herself. He didn't like to think he was a jealous person, but it didn't sit right at all that Darcy would share his bed with him but not her secrets. "It, um, just sort of came out when I carjacked him and…" His eyes widened and she slumped in defeat. "Okay, I made some really big mistakes in judgment, but my motives were pure. I needed to know if he was a Devotee or not, and having someone on my side sounded like a really good idea."

"I'm on your side," he countered quietly, stung that she'd thought she couldn't come to him with her fears. "Have I said or done something that would make you think that I wouldn't be?"

She shook her head. "Not exactly. I'm sorry. I was being…afraid and stupid. I should've trusted you, Rafe. I *do* trust you. Does that count for something now?"

"Of course it does. I just wish you could've felt this

way before you put yourself in danger. What if McCall had been a Devotee?"

"I'd have been screwed," she admitted sheepishly. "But he wasn't, so I dodged a bullet and recognized that I shouldn't have gone that route. Trust me, I wanted to tell you, but by then I didn't know how to bring it up."

"How about, 'Rafe, I need to talk to you. I'm Samuel Grayson's daughter'? That would've piqued my interest at the very least."

"This isn't funny, so don't make jokes," she said.

"Who's joking? Darcy…for future reference…just come out and tell me. I don't like surprises."

She nodded. That seemed fair. "Okay. Well, then, along those lines, I have something else to tell you."

He regarded her warily. "Yes?"

Get ready for bombshell number two. "I think I might be pregnant."

Chapter 23

The bottom dropped out of Rafe's world at Darcy's news. Well, the second bit of news, actually.

"Pregnant?" he repeated and she nodded. The night they'd went without a condom came rushing back and he groaned, kicking himself all over again for being so reckless. "I'm so sorry…"

She straightened, frowning. "Sorry? What do you mean, sorry?"

"It's my fault. I should've insisted on a condom. I know you said that it's difficult to get pregnant and, yes, if you look at the science, it seems the odds are stacked against human beings, but history has proven otherwise—getting pregnant is what a woman's body is designed to do."

She sniffed. "Well, my body wasn't. I never thought that was in my plan. However, now I'm not so sure and I don't want you apologizing. I've been thinking about it and, well, maybe it wouldn't be such a bad thing, after all."

"Darcy, you can't stay here if you're pregnant," Rafe said, his voice urgent. "I couldn't stand the thought of you and our child being in danger. It's bad enough that I'm worried sick about Devin. I can't do that with you."

She framed his face. "We're a team, Rafe. Without me, you'd be hiding in broom closets without so much as a flashlight. You're the brains but I'm the common sense of this operation. Without each other, we'd be in a mess. We need each other."

"I don't know," he said darkly. "I couldn't protect Devin or his mother. I can't fail with you. It would kill me."

"You won't."

He loved her conviction, that she believed in him wholly. It buoyed him even when he knew he ought to send her anywhere but here. He pulled her to him and held her tight. "I love you, Darcy."

"I know," she said through a watery giggle. "But before we start picking out nursery colors, we should take a test first. I'm only a week late and with all the stress…you know how it goes."

He nodded. "But I want you to know, either way, I'm here for you."

"Good. I'd hate to think that you'd drop me like a hot potato in case it turned out I wasn't knocked up." She grinned and he laughed.

"No. Not that kind of guy."

"I know that, too," she said softly, her eyes shining. "Now let's shake some damn trees and see if we can't find someone who knows something about Devin. Devin deserves his family."

"Tell me more about your biological mother," Rafe said later that evening. She had her feet propped on his legs and he was giving her a good foot massage.

Sighing, she said, "There's not a lot to tell. I don't know anything aside from her name and where she's from."

"Tell me what you know."

"Well, according to my adoptive mother, they met in foster care when they lived in Horn's Gulch. She only ever knew her as Catherine and she was younger than my adoptive mom. Once Catherine gave birth, she got real scared and made Louise promise she'd take care of me and keep me away from Samuel."

"Horn's Gulch, that's not too far from here," Rafe noted. "Did you ever take a drive there?"

"No. I thought about it, but I chickened out. I didn't know where to start and figured whatever leads had been there were likely long gone by now."

"If she was in foster care, it's likely there are records."

"Yeah, but aren't they sealed?" she asked.

"There are ways around that. I could make some calls if you like."

"Would you? I'd appreciate that," she said, smiling. He continued to rub her toes. She snuggled deeper into the sofa.

"How'd you feel when you found out that you were adopted?"

Darcy thought for a moment, remembering. "Sad. Not because I had a bad childhood or anything, but because I never got the chance to know Catherine. I wish I knew if we were alike or if our mannerisms were the same. I don't even know my own medical history. Yeah, so mostly sad."

He nodded and continued to rub. The motion soothed her, even though her heart hurt when she thought of Catherine and the loss of the only mother she'd ever known. "I miss my adoptive mother, though," she admitted in a tight voice. "We were very close. I was an only child and we were each other's support system. I'd always assumed it was because she'd been a single mom, but it was because she was always looking over her shoulder, afraid that Samuel would show up on her doorstep to take me away. I realize now that she shouldered a very heavy burden for me and my biological mother."

"She must've loved you both very much," he said quietly and she agreed.

"Yes. I know she did. And I miss her terribly." Her voice broke and he stopped rubbing to reach over and gather her in his arms. He held her that way so she could quietly cry, letting the grief she'd held back for too long wash over her. After a time, she wiped her nose with a tissue he'd handed her and she said, chuckling at the irony, "My mom would've loved you. She'd always said I ought to start dating doctors. She had this thing about wanting to know if my dates would be good providers down the line. I didn't have the heart to tell her that I wasn't dating those other guys as settle-down material. I was just looking for a good time."

"Is that what you thought when you saw me?" Rafe joked.

She lifted her head, a small smile on her face. "Not at first. You seemed kind of stiff. But that all changed within seconds of talking to you. I realized you had something special. And I was not above wanting to get into your pants, I won't lie."

"Are you saying you seduced me?" Rafe asked in mock indignation. She straddled him and he slid into a more comfortable spot with his hands cradling her backside. "I don't quite remember it that way."

"No? For a doctor you have a terrible memory," she teased and leaned into him for a deep kiss, reminding him just how easily she'd twisted him around her finger that first night.

"Ah," he said, a little breathlessly. "It's all coming back to me now, but how about a recap?"

"My pleasure. It went something like this…."

Rafe spent considerable time on the phone, even enlisting the help of Agent Hawk Bledsoe to track down some information on Catherine, but the foster mother who'd taken in young Catherine and Louise was long dead.

He shared the news with Darcy, wishing he'd had something more solid to lead with.

The light dimmed in her eyes, but she nodded. "I knew it was a long shot. So much time has passed. Thank you for checking, though."

He hated seeing her so despondent. He knew how that felt. "We'll keep trying. Any lead that comes along, we'll chase it down. I promise."

She took his hand and kissed his palm. "You're a good man, Rafe Black."

"So some say," he murmured, wishing he'd had better news. But there was something else he needed to know from her. "Did you take the second test?" he asked, his nerves taut. The first pregnancy test had been inconclusive, which could've meant, yes, she was pregnant or, no, she wasn't. They'd had to wait a few more days to take the test again.

"I did," she admitted, her mouth trembling a little. "It was negative."

He should've felt relief. But he didn't. "How do you feel about it?" he asked, wanting her perspective first. "Are you happy?"

She shrugged in answer. "I suppose. I mean I should be."

"But?"

"But I kind of got used to the idea and I liked it."

He smiled. "Me, too."

She looked up. "Really?"

"Yeah."

Darcy jumped into his arms. "You're constantly surprising me in a good way, not a scary or irritating sort of way." He laughed and kissed her. "So what does this mean?"

"It means I would've been overjoyed to have a child with you and when it happens for real, I know what a blessing it will be."

"I agree," she said, her laughter fading. "But I want to wait. I'm not entirely ready just yet."

"I'm glad we're on the same page. I want to focus on Devin for now. Later, we'll have a basketball team of kids."

"Whoa, now, let's not go crazy. One or two sounds doable...not a team of Globetrotters," she said, the laughter returning.

"Okay, it's up for negotiation, but for the time being, we agree."

"Yes."

They snuggled and spent the rest of the evening quiet and reflective, but beneath the coziness of the moment, each was processing everything in different ways. For Rafe, knowing Darcy wasn't pregnant relieved some pressure, but the knowledge that Devin was still missing weighed on him more heavily with each passing day.

If something didn't happen soon, he would lose his mind and do something crazy.

He had no idea that by tomorrow morning, his life was about to change.

* * *

Ford McCall entered the station early and something caught his eye. He stopped at Chief Fargo's office and saw a car seat on the desk. That in itself was something to make him stop in his tracks. Fargo didn't have kids. He walked in and went straight to the seat and found a note taped to it. "Little Devin Black belongs with his father. I found him all alone when Abby vanished and thought he was all alone in the world. Then when Dr. Black came to town, I loved little Devin too much to let him go. But I must do what's right."

Ford stared at the note, turning it over, searching for a signature, but it was simply a typed note, as impersonal as it was suspicious.

Fargo entered the room, carrying a dark-haired baby boy as awkwardly as if he'd been carrying a wiggling ferret. "Oh, I see you've found what was on my doorstep early this morning," he said sourly.

"Is that...Rafe Black's baby?" Ford asked, incredulous.

"It's what the note says, isn't it?" Fargo snapped, handing off the kid with distaste. "I'll do the honors and call Black. You keep the kid busy. He smells funky. Maybe you could check his pants."

Ford stared at the baby, unable to fathom that Baby Devin, the kid whose very existence had been questioned repeatedly for months, was now in his arms. He eyed Fargo, not buying for a second that the kid had just shown up without warning, but as he adjusted the baby, who'd begun to fuss, he realized now was not the time to pick that fight. He'd have to tell Hawk his suspicions later.

Fargo picked up the phone and made the call to Rafe without a lot of ceremony.

"Hey, Doc. I've got good news. Your kid showed up. I'll deliver him to your office in about a half hour." He hung up and met Ford's incredulous stare. "What? It's good news. He ought to be happy."

"Sure, Chief. It's good news," he said, patting the baby on his bottom when he fussed some more. "Doesn't it seem a little coincidental that the baby just showed up when Rafe put some pressure on you to find him?" he asked, unable to keep his suspicion to himself. "Just saying... seems odd."

Fargo's stare narrowed. "The kid's here. Rafe's happy. Case closed. Move on."

"Yeah, that's the Cold Plains way, isn't it?" he muttered, walking away from Fargo before he said something he really couldn't take back.

He supposed Fargo was right about one thing: Rafe would be happy and relieved. And that was a good thing. Ford would try to accept the news as simply that: good.

Rafe's hands shook as he clicked off his phone. Darcy stared, worried. "What's wrong?" she asked.

"That was Fargo. They've found Devin."

"What?" Darcy exclaimed. "Where?"

"I don't know. He didn't give me details. He's on his way now." Tears of joy brimmed in his eyes. "I'm finally going to meet my son, after all these long months, I'm finally going to meet him!"

Darcy rose and hugged him tightly. "I'm so glad, sweetheart. So glad. You deserve happiness. And Devin will be a lucky boy to have you as a father."

Rafe didn't have a chance to answer, for Fargo and Grayson both entered the office. Fargo was carrying a small baby boy.

The air squeezed from his lungs in a painful exhale; his heart hammered so hard he thought he might die on the spot. Darcy took a spot behind him, and Grayson's stare narrowed when he saw her. The meeting between the two momentarily took his attention as he worried that Grayson might recognize something familiar about Darcy, but Grayson gave nothing away. He simply smiled with generosity, like a king granting a full pardon to an unruly subject, and basked in Rafe's joy.

"Here," Fargo said, putting the boy unceremoniously into Rafe's arms. "Congratulations. It's a boy."

Grayson stepped forward, his arms outstretched as if to embrace Rafe and the baby, but he simply smiled and clapped his hands together as if with happiness. "Behind the scenes, I had Chief Fargo chasing down every lead, putting some heat on people of interest, but we didn't want to say anything until the investigation yielded results. And now, your son is in your arms. All's well that ends well, Dr. Black. Wouldn't you agree?"

Rafe barely heard Grayson, he was too busy taking in every detail of Devin's little face. "He's beautiful," he murmured, tears breaking the surface and starting to flow. He blinked them back and choked on the words he said next. "Thank you for bringing him home to me."

Fargo's smile bordered on a smirk, and Grayson simply looked smug, but Rafe didn't care. He had his son. He'd deal with the who, what and how later.

"Rest assured we haven't given up on finding who took the little guy," Grayson said, nodding to Fargo. "Isn't that right, Chief?"

"Absolutely," Fargo said, no doubt lying through his teeth. "Whoever did this will be caught. I promise you that."

Rafe looked up and met Fargo's stare. "Good. Because anyone who would steal a child is beyond redemption in my book."

"Well, you two have a lot of catching up to do. One more thing," Grayson said, going to the door. "What did you decide, on the offer to run the OB clinic?"

Rafe straightened and adjusted the baby in his arms. "I'm sorry, I have to decline. I like working with my patients too much here in my practice, but I'd be happy to continue volunteering on Saturdays to help out."

Darcy interjected with a sweet smile, "Plus now that we have Devin, our time will be limited. Isn't that right, sweetheart?"

Rafe caught Darcy's gaze and nodded in full agreement, in spite of Grayson's obvious displeasure at his refusal. "I plan to be a hands-on father. To this boy and any other that may come along."

Darcy beamed and shot Grayson a look that could only be deemed as a victory dance in her eyes. Grayson's smile tightened and he shrugged. "Understandable. But maybe with time, you'll change your mind. Until then...enjoy your son."

Rafe stared at the cherubic face that was so like his own and murmured a promise as he nuzzled the sweet, soft skin of his son, "Oh, I will."

The days that followed Devin's return were a whirlwind of activity. Darcy had a blast shopping for baby furniture and all the appropriate trappings, turning the guest bedroom into Devin's.

Rafe stared in wonder at the transformation. The room was painted in shades of baby blue with stenciled airplanes flying along the walls and a beautiful cherrywood crib set with matching bedding that filled the small room perfectly.

Darcy fell into the role of mother quite easily and was nearly as protective of Devin as Rafe, and it filled Rafe's heart with joy.

"Will you marry me?" he asked one morning after she'd fed and changed Devin. She paused in her dressing of the little man and stared. He realized he could've finessed it a bit more, but he was overcome with love for this woman and the words simply spilled out of their own accord. But no matter, it was his heart's desire in spite of the presentation. "I don't have a ring yet, but we can rectify that today if you like. All I know is that I want you in my life forever and the best way to do that is to give you my name. Would you do me the honor of being my wife and Devin's mother?"

It took an agonizingly long moment for Darcy to respond, and for a second, Rafe worried she'd turn him down, but that wasn't the case. She jerked a short nod, tears filling her eyes. "Yes," she whispered. "Nothing would make me happier." She glanced down at Devin and smiled. "I don't need a fancy ring. This little man is better than any material item you could give me. And I definitely want more of them. Maybe not this minute, but we can negotiate that basketball team."

He gathered her in his arms and held her close, sending a prayer to whoever might be listening to watch over them, for they'd need all the guardian angels out there to make it in Cold Plains.

Nothing had changed—Grayson still needed to be stopped and Rafe had vowed to help in any way that he could to find answers about Catherine—but with Darcy and Devin, he felt he could do anything.

It was the best feeling he'd had since stepping foot in Cold Plains, and he planned to savor it.

Epilogue

A commotion in the front office brought Rafe running. Darcy was helping a badly beaten woman into Exam Room One, galvanizing him into action.

The woman, face swollen and bruised, her lip and nose busted, groaned as she lay on the exam bed, holding her side. Rafe was horrified by the extent of her injuries, but the professional in him was already assessing her condition.

"Ma'am, can you tell me what happened?" he asked, swiftly checking her pupils for evidence of shock, then slipping a blood-pressure cuff on. "You're hurt badly. I'm going to stabilize you, but you need to go to the hospital."

She groaned again, tears squeezing from her swollen lids. "Hurtsss," she moaned. "So b-bad."

Rafe looked to Darcy and she shot off to call the ambulance.

"What's your name?" he asked, trying to keep her conscious. "I'm Dr. Black. I'm going to take care of you. You're safe now."

"G-Gemma," she managed to whisper, though it was difficult to understand at first because of her injured lip.

"Gemma? Okay, Gemma, the ambulance is here. I—" Her hand clutched his in a surprisingly strong grip. Her expression pleaded with him not to leave her. Fear was in her eyes and he nodded in understanding. "I'll go with you to the hospital." Her grip loosened as her eyes registered relief. Rafe couldn't help but wonder if this was the work of Grayson or his henchmen, but there was no way to find out at the moment. Gemma was barely conscious.

The ambulance arrived and trundled Gemma into the back, and Rafe climbed in to sit beside her.

"Cancel all patients," he instructed Darcy just before the doors closed, and they raced the short distance to the hospital.

He relinquished her care to the trauma department but he waited for news. It was an hour before they'd patched her enough to put her in a room, with heavy painkillers on a drip. Rafe entered her room, relieved to see the blood wiped away and the wounds attended to. He checked her chart. Severe facial lacerations and bruising, a bruised kidney and liver but otherwise no internal bleeding, which surprised him.

Rafe went to her bedside and found her awake.

"You should be resting," he said softly.

"Thank you," she said, her voice raspy and drugged.

"No need for thanks," he said. "I wouldn't be much of a doctor if I ignored an injured woman who stumbled into my practice."

She attempted a smile, but it was too painful and she stopped.

"Gemma, what happened?" he asked.

Just then Grayson walked in and Rafe resisted the urge

to scowl. Fargo must've alerted him to the call that went out over dispatch when the ambulance was called.

"I came as soon as I heard," Grayson said, his face a mask of concern. "Who did this?"

Rafe answered, "Not sure. Do you know her?"

Grayson shook his head and gingerly took her hand. "No, but she's in Cold Plains's care and we will do our best to find out who did this to her and bring them to justice."

Gemma stared at Grayson, her eyes brimming. "My ex-husband…he found me. I tried to run, but he caught me and did this…. He's dangerous…."

Grayson rubbed her hand gently. "Don't you worry about him. We'll find him before he can be a danger to anyone else. You rest."

Her eyelids fluttered shut and she dropped into a drugged sleep that she desperately needed to heal. Grayson turned to Rafe, who was watching the exchange with guarded reserve. He didn't trust Grayson taking an interest in this poor woman. She'd clearly been through enough. But he could say nothing. He was still walking a tightrope with Grayson, playing the part that kept him alive.

"Have the nurses tell me as soon as she's well enough to leave. I want to make sure she's taken care of. I will personally see to her needs. Cold Plains is a safe place. If word of this gets out, it could tarnish our image. This is a family-friendly town, not one where defenseless women get brutalized."

Amazingly hypocritical, thought Rafe but nodded gravely just the same. "Of course."

"I'll get Chief Fargo to take her statement when she's feeling up to it." Grayson took one last look at Gemma and said, "I'll bring the audio version of my lecture tonight— Healing the Heart. It's appropriate, don't you think?"

"Very," he agreed. "I think she'll like that."

Pleased, Grayson nodded and left.

As soon as Grayson was gone, Rafe dropped the act and regarded the sleeping Gemma with apprehension. Grayson taking an active interest in the woman wasn't a good thing. In his experience, when Samuel Grayson took a shine to a woman...sometimes they ended up dead.

He'd have to find a way to warn the woman...or else she'd find herself running from one madman—straight into the arms of another.

That now-familiar tightening in his chest reminded him that even though he'd finally found Devin, all was far from well in Cold Plains.

Rafe could feel the tension in the tightrope he continued to walk. The urge to pack up his little family and split was strong, but when he looked at Gemma, saw the trust in her eyes for the madman pretending to care about her well-being, he saw countless other people falling for Grayson's lies and he couldn't walk away. Not yet.

The battle was coming and, whether he liked it or not, he was already on the front lines.

There was no turning back now.

* * * * *

SUSPENSE

Harlequin® ROMANTIC
SUSPENSE

COMING NEXT MONTH
AVAILABLE MARCH 27, 2012

#1699 CAVANAUGH'S BODYGUARD
Cavanaugh Justice
Marie Ferrarella

#1700 LAWMAN'S PERFECT SURRENDER
Perfect, Wyoming
Jennifer Morey

#1701 GUARDIAN IN DISGUISE
Conard County: The Next Generation
Rachel Lee

#1702 TEXAS BABY SANCTUARY
Chance, Texas
Linda Conrad

REQUEST YOUR FREE BOOKS!
2 FREE NOVELS PLUS 2 FREE GIFTS!

❦ Harlequin®

ROMANTIC
SUSPENSE

Sparked by Danger, Fueled by Passion.

HRS11B

Taft Bowman knew he'd ruined any chance he'd had for happiness with Laura Pendleton when he drove her away years ago...and into the arms of another man, thousands of miles away. Now she was back, a widow with two small children...and despite himself, he was starting to believe in second chances.

Harlequin Special® Edition® presents a new installment in USA TODAY *bestselling author RaeAnne Thayne's miniseries,* THE COWBOYS OF COLD CREEK.

Enjoy a sneak peek of
A COLD CREEK REUNION

Available April 2012 from Harlequin® Special Edition®

A younger woman stood there, and from this distance he had only a strange impression, as though she was somehow standing on an island of calm amid the chaos of the scene, the flashing lights of the emergency vehicles, shouts between his crew members, the excited buzz of the crowd.

And then the woman turned and he just about tripped over a snaking fire hose somebody shouldn't have left there.

Laura.

He froze, and for the first time in fifteen years as a firefighter, he forgot about the incident, his mission, just what the hell he was doing here.

Laura.

Ten years. He hadn't seen her in all that time, since the week before their wedding when she had given him back his ring and left town. Not just town. She had left the whole damn country, as if she couldn't run far enough to get away from him.

Some part of him desperately wanted to think he had made some kind of mistake. It couldn't be her. That was just some other slender woman with a long sweep of honey-blond hair and big, blue, unforgettable eyes. But no. It was definitely Laura. Sweet and lovely.

Not his.

He was going to have to go over there and talk to her. He didn't want to. He wanted to stand there and pretend he hadn't seen her. But he was the fire chief. He couldn't hide out just because he had a painful history with the daughter of the property owner.

Sometimes he hated his job.

Will Taft and Laura be able to make the years recede...or is the gulf between them too broad to ever cross?

Find out in
A COLD CREEK REUNION
Available April 2012 from Harlequin® Special Edition®
wherever books are sold.

Celebrate the 30th anniversary
of Harlequin® Special Edition® with a bonus story
included in each Special Edition® book in April!